GARI

Enjoy this
book

Diana
Bettinson

Diana Bettinson

Acknowledgements

Many thanks to:

My husband for his mechanical knowledge

Suzan Collins for her support

Proof reader: John Bettinson

Dedication

To my family who have been forced to read much of the book at the various stages of writing.

THE DREAD

As the pale light of dawn crept across the sky, Gari became aware of his appalling circumstances. It was true, the dread, that had haunted him for so long. The dread that had dominated his every waking thought and invaded his dreams.

He was in the killing place. Here, where cars were brought to be put down, painfully. To die, to have what life was left, ended. He was not to be allowed to fade away gently he would go in the most horrible way.

To his right Gari saw a huge crowd of cars, to his left there was just a pile of metal cubes. These were once fine vehicles, the pride of their owners. Now they were no longer wanted. They were all crushed and even more indignity was to come. They would all be melted down. These cubes were already dead; they were the lucky ones; their pain was over.

Ahead he saw a crane from which dangled a giant grabbing claw. The claw attacked from above; there was no escape. It clenched the car round the roof breaking any windows that were still in place, lifting it in this excruciating manner and swinging it into the jaws of the killing machine.

All those stories that had been told to wayward, young cars were true; not fable.

The crusher stood with its monstrous mouth gaping wide open ready for another car to be dropped in. the mouth would close first the sides, then the ends.

Finally; a lid closed over the trapped vehicle in an evil hug of death. There was no getting away, their batteries had been removed, just the inexorable squeezing, shaping into those lifeless cubes.

It was unnaturally quiet in the yard. None of the cars felt in the mood to talk and of course no noise came from the cubes. The cars were all too frightened to speak, some gave the odd groan, some whimpered but for the most part the place was silent.

The men had come for Gari under the cover of dark; they had dragged him from the nice warm barn he had been pushed into only recently. They shooed the chickens out of his cab, and pulled him onto a trailer. He had hoped to be safe in the barn to rot into a peaceful death alone, not lonely as he had his memories. His hopes were cruelly dashed and now he could only stare at the crusher with gruesome fascination. Knowing, at last what his fate was and how his ending was to come.

Work starts early in a scrap yard, it was not long before the humans arrived. One started up the crane; one went to the controls of the crusher and yet more began to strip cars of their useful parts.

'Hey, Bob, give us a hand to shift this mini will you?'

Two men came to Gari and pushed him over to the fence.

'This one's sold. Some bloke's coming for it.'

Gari felt a shudder of hope run from his front bumper to his exhaust pipe. He stood by the fence watching, waiting. He watched the crane lowering, the claw make a grab. He saw a car swing over the mouth. He witnessed a cube roll out of the end of the killing machine. A great sadness came over him, there was nothing he could do to help and nothing could ease the pain. He couldn't watch any more of this vehicle killing; he would look at the young cars on the road and remember his own youth.

Later that day, a tractor and trailer squelched across a muddy farmyard with its precious load, and slithered to a halt outside a barn. Gari was in a state of shocked disbelief, he was the precious load. He was away from the scrap yard and was still alive.

'You got it then, Dad?' Marc asked as he walked from the barn wiping his hands on an oily cloth.

'Yes, but I had to give them £50 for it,' said Nick.

'Is Jon about, we need him to get it down off the trailer and into the barn before your Mum sees it.'

'He's in the orchard with Ruth feeding the horses. I'll get them both. Best be getting those number plates off before Mum comes out to have a look.' Mark said over his shoulder as he walked to the paddock.

'That's better, those number plates were hurting' Gari thought to himself he then felt ropes being untied and as the back board of

7

the trailer was being let down, some planks were wedged under his wheels. He was rolled backwards off the trailer and then forwards into the barn.

'Look out here comes Mum.'

'It's okay, the plates are off, she won't recognise it.'

'This little project of yours is going to take some time by the looks of it then Nick.' Spoke a voice from behind him. 'Oh, you didn't tell me it was a green one, same colour as Gari.'

Gari knew that voice. It's Lucy, his first owner. He would know her anywhere. He waited for her to walk round to the front so he could see per properly. He never thought he would see her again, Oh the joy! She looked older, but then of course she did, she was years older and had grown up children now. When Gari first knew her he was a new car and she was a young girl. Tall slim with long blond hair, blue eyes and to Gari the most beautiful person he had ever known.

'That's all right Mum, while Dad is busy with the car I will run the farm for him' said Ruth, the only other female there.

She looked like the young Lucy that Gari knew all those years ago.

'You can keep your sticky fingers off my farm young lady,' said Nick.

Marc had already lifted Gari's bonnet to have a look at the engine. 'Hmm, best thing we can do here is drop the engine and sub frame complete, then I can take a look at it,' he mumbled.

'You're the mechanic Marc, Jon is in charge of the body work,' Nick replied,

'Well it needs a new sub frame at the back here for a start.'

'Oh yes, now that he mentioned it there was a pain in the rear sub frame area' thought Gari.

'Well lunch is ready and as this is still a working farm. The car will have to wait for another day,' said Lucy.

They stood for a minute to look at Gari and he had a chance to have a good look at them. He tried to keep the smile from showing but was not sure he succeeded that well. He was so happy. Here was Lucy and Nick the first people he had ever really known and their children. Marc, Jon and Ruth, who looked so much like her mother that Gari thought he must have been transported back in time. He stood there reminiscing for the rest of the day and was humming a happy tune to himself and telling himself how lucky he was.

'There I was just this morning in the scrap yard, about to be crushed to death and now look where I am, in a nice dry barn.'

'Don't be thinking about that old yard. Nick has been after you for a long while' a gruff voice told him.

'Oh I'm sorry I didn't realise I was thinking aloud, I do a lot of that because I have been alone for a long while. Did you say Nick has wanted me for a long while? I knew him years ago and Lucy of course.'

'That I do know, Nick has told everyone about you except Lucy. She can't know just yet, you've got to be done up first.'

'Done up? Like new? Is that possible?'

'Of course it's possible. I'm Trevor, by the way, the farm tractor and I know you is Gari, what I don't know is how come you're called Gari and not something beginning with 'M' ?'

'That's easy, my number is Gar I C. Lucy said that Gary Cooper was a film star and that I was her little Car Star, what with me being a Mini Cooper: so she called me Gari. She was proud of me then,' said Gari with a sigh.

'She will be proud of you again, but how did you know her in the first place?'

'Well I was built in a place called Lonbridge near Birmingham and I cost £756 when I was new and that included tax,' the salesman said. 'I don't know what tax is but no-one seems to like it. I was driven from Lonbridge to Chelmsford with some smart red number plates on. I stood, proud in the middle of the indoor showroom and that is where I first met Lucy.'

She came to the place to buy me. That was in 1965 so that is sort of my birthday. How long have you been here Trevor?'

'Oh I don't rightly know, but I think I came here millennium year.'

'Well I am a good bit older than you are and I look it, but not for long hey? I am going to look like new; oh I can hardly believe it is possible. I am so tired and broken I don't see how I will ever have the energy I used to have.'

'Of course you will, Marc is good with engines he'll get you going again.'

But Trevor noticed he was talking to himself, all the excitement had made Gari very sleepy.

ACHES AND PAINS

Gari awoke with a start, someone had opened his driver's door and it dropped down. Jon then opened the passenger door and it almost fell off completely.

'Well Ruth,' he said 'that means both 'A' panels need replacing. I had better see if I can get those doors off without doing too much damage. Can you be taking the seats out?'

'Sure, no problem,' she replied.

Marc was having trouble opening the boot, the handle was rusted tight. When he did get it open he lifted out the old battery and then unscrewed the boot lid. Nick meanwhile was taking off the bonnet.

With each part that came off Gari felt all his aches and pains easing away. There he stood no doors, no bonnet, and no boot lid. He felt somewhat undressed. The windows came out next, and then all these parts were carefully lined up against the back wall of the barn.

Nick began to examine each one. 'Some of these will need replacing but you should be able to repair most of them Jon.'

'Just one question Dad,' asked Ruth, 'would you be doing all of this if you didn't have, not, one but two car types in the family?'

She was busy yanking out the filthy rotten carpet. Marc and Jon both worked in a garage not far away. They had both started there when they left school, Jon in the body shop and Marc was a mechanic.

'It would have made the job more difficult but not impossible,' Nick answered with a smile.

'What we need now is a trolley jack,' called Marc, 'if we can lift up the front end and put it on stands then the engine and front sub frame should drop out nicely. Just go and get it for me, will you Ruth?'

'Trolley Jack,' mused Ruth 'is that the big pumpy thing that lifts things up?'

Marc laughed, walked over and patted her on top of her head and said 'My, what a clever girl she is, now off you go and fetch it'.

Jon and Nick stood and clapped their hands and as she left the barn she turned and took a bow. Gari was so happy to see all these antics, to be part of the family again; it gave him a nice warm, wanted feeling.

Lifting Gari up on the jack was not hard but when it came to undoing the nuts and bolts that held in his sub frame, well that was a different matter. They were all rusted on tight.

The rear sub frame was a problem as well, but eventually Gari found a much reduced remainder of himself standing on a pallet.

There were chalk marks all over what was left of his bodywork.

When Trevor came in that night, he couldn't believe his eyes. 'OHH you are all in bits and all over the barn.'

'They are all the parts that need replacing or welding,' Gari told him. 'Jon is going to do lots of work on me, and take away all the hurting bits and ease my old aches.'

'Well you look happier and that's a fact.'

'Oh I feel very happy, there are only a few bits that hurt now, I never realised how much pain there was with all them broken bits, and Jon says he'll be able to sort out some new ones soon.'

'Yes I heard him tell Nick. Marc is taking your engine into work to sort it out there. By the time those boys have finished you will be like a new car. Want to tell me some more of your life story?'

'Right, you know I told you about the day my number plates were put on on my birthday, well that was the day that Lucy came for me. She was nearly as excited as I was, I could feel it as she drove me away from the garage. Anyway we went quite a distance and guess where we ended up? On a farm. Quite a big farm and when we stopped Lucy ran into the house. Very soon some people came out with her and stood around me.

'Would they be Lucy's parents then?' asked Trevor.

'Yes, they were really nice. I was a bit nervous but said that I was a lovely colour, what size my engine was and things like that. Nick was there, he came over and lifted my bonnet, and he was very interested in my engine, what with it being bigger than most Mini engines. Lucy and Nick decided that they had time to go for a drive. 'Lets go to the coast' Lucy said 'you can drive if you like'.

It was on that drive that Lucy gave me my name, and something else happened on that drive, something really nice. Nick proposed to Lucy.

'What? asked Trevor.

'Right here in my cab he asked her to marry him. We had got to the beach by the time he got the words out and they went running and dancing all around the beach.'

'AHHH, that's nice, gives me a warm glow,' said Trevor.

'Well I just felt embarrassed, I thought it was a good job there was no-one else about to see these crazy humans dancing all over the beach on a cold day in January.

Anyway, Nick had found a farm he wanted to buy, this one in fact. They decided to settle here with Nick working the farm as best as he could and Lucy doing her hairdressing in people's homes to make some more money.

Things were tight, money was short but they worked hard and did the house up so it would be ready for them to live in. Lucy and I didn't live here then, not until after the wedding, but we came over every day and I brought lots of stuff to make the house nice.

When Lucy and Nick got married I took Lucy to the church. I know people usually have big posh cars for that, Rolls Royce's and the like but Lucy insisted that she wanted to go in her very own car. That was a very nice day and I felt proud as punch. I was all polished up and had white ribbons fixed to my bonnet and my mirrors and doors. Lucy had a bit of a problem getting into my cab and even more of one getting out because of her big white dress. It was very wide with huge skirts and a long train, but she made it in the end much to the amusement of the guests.

Her Dad drove us and he was always pushing her dress out of the way of my gear stick. Everyone had a good laugh about it and I was giggling all the way to the reception although I didn't take Lucy there, a big car took both her and Nick. George, Lucy's brother drove me there, that was the first time he had driven me, but that's another story.

When the reception was nearly over George came out to me with another man. They were carrying boxes which they loaded into my boot and on my back seats. Then they started to blow up a whole load of balloons which they literally filled my cab with. George wrote some words on my back screen. 'Just Married', it was and I had seen it on other cars, never thought I would have it written on my screen.

Then they tied ribbons to any bit of me they could and then, strangest of all they tied some boots and cans to my back bumper, on a long piece of cord.

Lucy laughed like mad when she saw what they had done to me and when she and Nick tried to get in to my cab with all those balloons. There were balloons floating everywhere and children chasing them all around. It was chaos, and noisy as everyone shouted 'Goodbye' and threw lots of little bits of paper all over us. Confetti it was called and it went everywhere. I was littered with the stuff but no-one seemed to mind. When we drove off I could hardly hear my engine what with the shouting and the rattle of the cans behind us. We didn't go very far before Nick stopped in a lay-by and Lucy and him began to clear me up a bit. They took a long while to do it because they kept stopping for a kiss and cuddle.

They rubbed the 'Just Married' off my back screen and eventually we went on our way, much cleaner and quieter.

The next stop was a place called Dover; we were going on a ferry to France.

'Honeymoon?' asked the man who came over to check the tickets and passports.

'How did you guess?' asked Nick 'I thought we had cleared all the evidence away.'

'Still some confetti in there, dead give-away that.'

'It will take forever to get rid of that, if we ever do,' said Lucy.'

Trevor interrupted 'Ruth did find some under your carpet, she nearly told Lucy about it.'

'Did she? OOPS! Lucy mustn't know yet, must she?'

Anyway it was strange in France; we had to drive on the other side of the road. We stopped for the night soon after we got off the ferry then I found out what was in the boxes. There was a tent and cooking gear, food and clothes. All the sort of things people need for camping out. The weather was nice and warm as it is in August, and as we drove down through France it got hotter.

Even with all my windows open and my fan working flat out, Lucy got very hot and sticky. We had to stop quite often for them to have a drink. They would go into churches and other large buildings, which cooled them down.

We often stopped to look at scenery; there are some very pretty parts of countryside in France.'

'They do still go there, they use to take the children when they were little.'

'Yes we went a couple of times.'

'That do seem a bit odd though don't it, they drive on the wrong side o the road, I wonder how a French tractor would feel over here?'

'Very strange I should think. I felt rather strange but we were not there long, just a couple of weeks. Then we came back and got to work.

I took all Lucy's hairdressing equipment to ladies houses so she could do their hair. And we went to the shops quite often. I got very friendly with some other cars that seemed to always go shopping at the same time as we did.'

There was one in particular. A Morris Minor who was a great friend of mine, he was called Maurice Chevalier. He was named after a French actor who had brought out a very popular film in 1958, which was the year he was built. I did hear that he still lives with the same people. I hope he is still in good condition, and happy.

Sometimes we would go to a big town to shop and after a while I noticed we were going more often. Lucy, I could see was getting bigger and she was having trouble getting out of my cab. We had been together for about two years when I heard something that brought my world crashing around my ears. Nick and Lucy were in the barn talking about me.

'When the baby comes I am going to need a bigger car, I will not be able to fit a carry cot and all my work into Gari.'

'I thought you would give up work when the baby came, will you have time and energy for both?' Nick teased her.

'Most of my customers have children, so the baby will be able to come with me. I will have to cut down on my hours a bit but there is no reason for me to give up. Anyway we still need the money to pay off the loan from the farm.'

'All right, if that is what you want we had better find a buyer for Gari, but I don't want you working too hard, we could manage you know.'

'I suppose we could manage but I don't want to just manage, even if it means losing Gari.'

They kissed and as Lucy walked out of the barn she patted my roof. I think it was the first time in my life that I ever cried. That night I cried and cried the whole night through. My whole world was coming to an end, I was being sent away from my home. Where was I going and would I ever see the farm again? Lucy and Nick were my people, we had fun together, now they didn't want me anymore. Where was I to go? What would happen to me? I cried for days and days, I nearly started a rust patch under my headlights. My screen washer bag was always empty. Lucy thought it had a leak and said she would have to get it fixed or they would never be able to sell me.

I tried to stop to please her; I thought that it was because I was miserable that she wanted to get rid of me. But I was so sad I just could not stop crying. Lucy said it was strange that the leak only started when they had talked about selling me.

Nick said that her pregnancy was giving her fanciful thoughts but she paid me extra attention all the same, which made me sadder still. One day I saw George with Nick walking towards me. George was younger than Lucy and taller. His hair was the same colour as hers and he looked very much like her. He sat in my driver's seat and pushed it back as far as it would go, Nick got in the other side and they took me out for a drive around the country lanes.

George drove me faster than I have ever been driven before.

We screamed round corners; sometimes we actually lost the road and slid. We nearly went off the road a few times. Nick told him to slow down but George just laughed. He said that he needed to know how I handled at high speed. I thought that all in all, he did rather well; I was very scared but excited as well. I hoped he would take me out again as it took my mind off the problems.

Little did I know?

I didn't see George again for about a week, then one day he drove into the yard in a much bigger car.

I remembered it from the wedding but had not seen it since then. It was my replacement, a Cortina, big enough for a carry cot and some boxes. I hated it; it was going to be Lucy's car instead of me. I couldn't look at it. I was crying again, I was so sad. I watched as Nick and George shake hands and swap keys. Nick then patted George on the shoulder and said 'I hope he wins for you.'

Lucy came over and put her hand on my roof and said 'Goodbye Gari, be good for George. Win him lots of prizes'. I couldn't think what she could possibly mean and to be honest I couldn't care less at the time.

George and I drove out of the yard, I wanted to scream at them to let me stay, my heart was breaking, and it was like a stabbing pain in my sump. I couldn't scream, I was too choked up. I felt so desolate as we drove away from the only home I had ever known. I sobbed and sobbed and felt sure that George would feel the juddering and take me back. But he didn't. No-one noticed that I was so sad and that I was crying. Nobody noticed because it was raining.'

SPECIAL STAGES

There was a beam above and just to the right of Gari in the barn, Nick and Marc with Jon's help fixed up a pulley arrangement to it. They then hoisted Gari's engine up in the air so that it was swinging from the beam. Nick went out but was soon back, at the wheel of the land rover. The engine was then lowered into the back of the land rover.

'That is about all we can do today, boys. If you take Lenny into work tomorrow with the engine Marc, then you can bring back the Mig Welder so Jon can be doing his bit with the bodywork,' said Nick.

'What are you going to do about the parts that we can't get from Taylor's?' asked Marc.

'I have a book indoors that has some addresses and phone numbers in, all dealers in new and used mini parts. I should be able to get all we need from there; I've still got my list.'

'I'll take this engine to work and should be able to take it apart tomorrow, a fine way to spend my holiday, working.'

'Well, Jon will be spending his holiday at home doing what he always does.'

'Yes,' said Jon, 'I love cutting up bodies.'

The three men laughed and Nick said 'Speaking of bodies, what was that you were trying to tell me about a new head for the engine Marc?'

'Well, to be able to use unleaded petrol the head will need to be changed. We can soon get one for it.'

Once the men left the barn Lenny the land rover introduced himself to Gari and then said 'I've herd lots about you, pal how are you settling in then? I'll tell you what though. You have got Boris worried. He is the family car and thinks you are here to replace him.'

'Oh dear, do you really think he was upset? I am sure that is not the plan at all, I thought I was supposed to be one of those 'Sunday cars'.'

'And so you are, pal and so you are but it don't hurt to shake up old Boris once in a while, it's a good laugh, just watching him getting angry He thinks he is better than the rest of us being the big luxury car he is. He is coming in tonight I think.'

So Gari had then met Lenny and in due course he met Boris, as much as he liked the land rover and the tractor, he found Boris somewhat frightening.

'What is all this, you are not even a whole car, and what is this mess all over the barn. It all belongs to you I suppose? Do we really have to live in this pigsty?'

'Come on Boris, no need to go upsetting him, he has had a tough enough time of it poor kid,' said Trevor.

'Kid, did you say kid? He is no kid he is old, I am a young car.' Boris retorted. Gari let Boris carry on for a while about how messy the barn was and if he got a scratch, Gari would be sorry. Boris would see to that.

'Young you may be but you have never learned any manners, and if you don't like the state of the barn, then stay out because this is my home now,' yelled Gari.

'Yes just calm down now Boris we have enough space for all of us.' said Lenny. Trevor nodded in agreement and Boris realised he was actually being mean for no good reason.

'Well I am not here to replace anyone: let's get that straight.' said Gari.

Right, then you can all stop arguing because I want to be hearing about Gari's time with George.

'So you were the rally car?' Boris asked in an apologetic way.

'Well I did do some rallies with George and Fiona.'

'Oh do tell us about it,' Boris asked.

STILL IN ONE PIECE

Jon was really rather busy, he had taken Gari's near side outer sill off and was about to cut away the rusty parts of his inner sills. This had all caused him some problems, because as we know Gari was not standing on his wheels but on a pallet. Jon had adapted the pallet so that he could work on him without too many obstructions, and of course he was working at floor level.

This is no way to work on a car he muttered to himself. I can do this but all the other work will have to wait until we can fit the new sub frames and I can get it back on its wheels.

Marc had brought home some sheet metal which Jon now started to cut bits out of so that he could weld them to Gari's bodywork, but as he tried to fit the pieces into place he noticed that what was left of the body of the car was bending.

'How's it going?' asked Nick as he walked into the barn.

'Not good, everything is bending because it is not supported, I'll prop it up all around and then we will just have to leave it until Marc has done the engine and transmission and we can put it all back together.'

'Is it bent very much? It's already been apart for a while.'

'No it only started going when I took off the sill. What are these holes in the boot? Looks like something has been bolted on here, there are some more at the top.'

'That must be where George bolted on a partition to block off the boot when he was rallying. It was all stripped out and made as light as possible.'

'This isn't the car he won his big rally in is it?'

'No he was in the Ford team when he won that one but he got a bit of practice in this one. Of course Fiona took a second place in the ladies section of one of the big Britain rallies.'

'I never knew Fiona was such a good driver, why didn't she carry on?'

'She said that she had done what she wanted to do, prove that she was a good driver and then was happy to support George in his driving.

Anyway it was about that time that they decided to marry and soon after the first of your many cousins arrived.'

'Motherhood took over from driving at breakneck speed round the country lanes then.'

'How very old fashioned, I never realised Aunt Fiona was so traditional,' said Ruth who had been standing there unnoticed.

'Things were different in the 70's, girls would get married and become housewives, not like my daughter who insists on being a farmer, and who would rather muck out pigs than wash up dishes.'

'Good thing to, but you see we can have the best of both worlds now-a-days. We can be whatever we want. As indeed Mum did, although her job is a very feminine one she has always worked and been a wife and a mother.'

'Yes but she was unusual, you might say she still is. It is a shame we cannot get on with this little job, I want to get it finished for the 19th of August, so that I can give it to her for our anniversary. There is also a classic car rally on the 25th of that month.'

'Oh yes, Peter Taylor is going to put his Morris Minor into that one,' said Jon.

'Maurice Chevalier, has he still got that?' asked Ruth.

'Had it since it was brand spanking new, when they stopped using it as the family car he tarted it up and now it only comes out if it is not raining. I often get to polish it for him, you can't say no to your boss can you?' Jon told them.

Gari was so excited when he heard this that he thought the humans would be sure to see him shivering. Not only did he have a date when he would be finished but he was going to see his old friend again, he had to tell someone.

In fact he was bursting to tell someone, if only Trevor would come in, he could tell him, or Boris or Lenny.

'Oh someone come and talk to me.' he thought.

Trevor did not come home until quite late that night but he knew that the little car was frantic to tell him something.

'Guess what?' Gari squealed as soon as they were alone, and he told the tractor all he had heard that morning.

'Well I'll be blowed, you mean that old Morris what do belong to Jon's boss do be the same as the one what you did know all them years ago?'

'Isn't it great, it's brilliant, it's it's...'

'I think you ad better be calming yourself down, or you be going to shake yourself off that pallet and where would you be? Right in the muck that's where.'

'You're right, as usual, I suppose I should try to calm down but I haven't felt this good since I was rallying with George and Fiona. I was going to tell you about that wasn't I?'

Gari took a deep shuddering breath and began.

We did some local rallies, with George driving and Fiona navigating. That meant she had to tell George when a bend or corner was coming up so he could just concentrate on driving as fast as he could for the conditions. You couldn't go too fast or you would have penalties.

The stages, as they were called were timed and had to be done with in the time that was set.

George use to miss the bends sometimes and each time I would spend the next few days in the workshop having dents bashed out. But as time went on he got better and sometimes we got all the way through a rally without having a crash at all. One though put me, George and Fiona out of a rally altogether. I was broken and had to be winched onto a lorry back to the workshop. That one hurt I can tell you. But all these were qualifying Rallies and when George and Fiona got good enough we were able to enter a really big rally.

We had to make our way to a big hotel in London, that's where we were to start from. We already had our numbers because George had sent his entrance fee in earlier. We were number 121. I found out that there are 156 entrants so we were fairly down the field.

The rally started at 7 o'clock on a Friday morning with one car leaving every minute, so we left at one minute past nine. There was someone famous there, I don't know who, but he was holding a flag which he brought down with a great sweep to start us off.

We drove north for a while to the first checkpoint, I don't know how far it was but it didn't seem to take long before George was stopping the car and Fiona went running to get the score card marked.

The road sections are not really that interesting, just like ordinary driving but not knowing where you are going.

But the special stages, well they were different. The first one was in Nottinghamshire, in a place called Sherwood Forest. There is a big wood there but not much of the actual Sherwood Forest left now. It was winter time and the forest was very frosty, all the puddles were frozen over and some of them were absolutely solid ice and they didn't break under my wheels.

As we went away from the checkpoint into the forest I remembered the last rally, when we crashed. Well I didn't want to do that again so I tried to go slowly but George would have none of that, he made me go really fast between all those tall trees.

There were people everywhere, all standing beside the track. It was roped off of course but they still stood so close that I almost touched one of them. The marshals were running around trying to make all the people stand back but they would not stay, they kept pushing forward to see the cars come through.

At first we had to go down a long straight track but it suddenly turned to the left, George did a superb handbrake turn, got us round the corner safely and hardly lost any speed at all.

Then we hit a patch of wet muddy stuff and my back end started to weave from side to side, George tried to correct it but he couldn't get it straight without slowing down. By now, with all the excitement I was trying to go much faster as well.

We started to go really well and I felt we were going to come out of this special stage without a mishap. Then on a stretch where there was a tall bank on one side of us and a ditch on the other, something fell down the bank.

One of the spectators had been holding a big bag. He slipped and fell, dropping his bag which fell down the bank right in front of us. George swerved over to miss it but then we hit another patch of thick gooey mud and started to slide. I watched a ditch coming closer and closer and then I knew we were going into it.

'No' I cried, 'No, I can't do that, I screamed, not the ditch' but hard as I tried I couldn't stop sliding. I knew I was going into that ditch and then my front wheels hit solid ground; George felt it as well and turned the steering wheel away. I knew that he and Fiona were holding their breath and I felt them both let out a big sigh as I turned away from the hateful ditch, but one of my rear wheels went into it and then the whole of my back end slid down.

All of a sudden the spectators who had been such a nuisance, all scrambled down the bank and into the ditch. It was very wet but they didn't seem to worry, they just lifted up my back end and put us back on the track.

Fiona waved at them to say thank you and we drove away very fast, spraying them all with mud as we went.

Round the next bend I saw the checkpoint and that was the first special stage of the rally over and I was still in one piece.

Back on the road, I noticed that we were sliding about more than normal. Fiona at first thought that something had broken but I could feel my wheels getting more grip. It was all the extra mud on my tyres that was making us slide like that. The road stages were for me a bit of a rest but very soon we came to another special one.

By the time we reached the second special stage the wind had blown up, Fiona said that the scrutinisers at the last checkpoint had told her it was gale force winds with gusts even harder in some places. Where do you think is the worst place for a car to be in a howling wind? We found ourselves out in the open on the Yorkshire Moors. A farmer had said we could use some of his land for this stage, it was wild and hilly and very windy. One time we caught up with another car, it was one like Boris, a BMW.

Being a bigger car it caught the wind even more than me and as we came up to it a gust of wind hit us. I was lucky, the wind just sort of brushed over my roof but the poor BMW got the full force of it and it just tipped over. Right in front of us it just went, well I couldn't believe it when I saw what was happening, it didn't seem possible to me that the wind could do that to a car but it had and there it was. Well George stopped me as quick as he could both he and Fiona got out and rushed over to it. The people were alright.

Of course they were wearing crash helmets and were completely strapped into their seats. They were climbing out of the near side door, which was now on top and they all stood there trying to decide how to get the car on its wheels again. By this time another car had come along and so there were two more people to help and they soon got it upright.

It started first turn of the engine, so soon we were all off again.'

'Did it go alright then, the BMW that weren't badly hurt then?'

'It was hurt but not bad enough to stop it from going on; I saw it later and had a chat when we had a rest stop. It was a she; and her name was Brenda, she was a good sport and passed off her dented side as if it didn't matter, the only thing she wanted to do was win the rally. She didn't win but she came in quite high up I think.

'I was moaning about a small pain I had at the time because George and Fiona rushed out of me to go to her they left both my doors open, the wind caught them and they both went back on themselves, the stoppers were broken and I had small dents in both my front wings where the doors hit. But when I was talking to Brenda later I realised I was moaning about nothing compared to her injuries. From then on I didn't let a little dent worry me; I decided that I wanted to win a rally.'

'Did you ever win one then?'

'No I never did but I did come second with Fiona one time. That was after George had joined a works team.'

'What's a works team then?'

'Well all the car manufacturers enter cars for the big rallies, it just helps to prove how good their cars are, and they have lots of back up mechanics and things to repair parts if they get broken. They have special drivers who sometimes get to be quite famous, because they spent most of the year driving rallies all over the world. George had come to the notice of the Ford team and they asked him to drive for them, in a big rally in Africa at first, and after that he drove for them in all the rallies for some years I think.'

'That doesn't seem right to me, what with them having mechanics and all that, don't seem fair that don't.'

'There is a different set of prizes for the works teams, and some special prizes for the people who enter privately, so we were no competing against the works team alone we could win the private section of the rally. Of course there is nothing to stop us from doing repairs where there is time. And the works teams did not have any more time that we did and sometimes the privately driven cars did win the rally but more usually it would be a works team. Anyway that is what George said when he was offered the place, and he would be getting paid to do what he liked doing best.'

There were no more big mishaps on this rally and we came in at the ninth place after nearly 1800 miles of driving.

We stopped for meal stops and only one night so we were going most of the time and we were all exhausted at the end. But we were very happy even to have finished, because out of all the cars that started only 70 got to the finish, which was less than half. I

was very proud and so were George and
Fiona.

HER NAME WAS MONICA

Jon found that he was getting on much better the next day because Marc had brought home some axle stands. This meant the three men could lift Gari up off the pallet with helpful, shouted instructions from Ruth and then he could do the work.

The sills were off and the inner sills were welded with new pieces of metal to make them solid which took away yet another pain. There were two new front wings propped up against the wall of the barn. Jon had welded on the outer sills which had arrived at the same time. He then cut out all the bad bits of Gari's inner wings and welded new metal onto them to make them all sound and strong again.

Before he knew what was happening Gari found that his body was all mended and feeling very new and strong.

Even the two little holes in his floor which had nagged at him with a niggling ache had been repaired.

So now although he still felt a bit undressed without his wings on he was strong and healthy again. Not a single pain did he feel. Jon stood back to check that he had done all the welding he needed to before he put on the new front wings.

If a car can smile then that is what Gari was doing when Trevor came in that night. Lenny came into the barn as well but Boris was taking Lucy and Nick out for the evening so he stayed outside the house.

'You're looking well pleased with yourself.' Lenny told him.

'I know. See those? They are my new doors over there and that is my new boot lid. Jon is going to put them on tomorrow and I have new 'A' panels now so the doors won't fall down anymore when somebody opens them.'

'What do them there 'A' panels do then boy?'

'You don't have them Trevor, as you've got no doors, they are the side bits that my doors are fixed to, where the hinges are. If only I had my engine and gear box I could go out for a run around, but then I need my wheels as well.'

'And lights, and bumpers, and loads more things you still haven't got yet, Pal.'

'Happen they going to put them fancy rally lights on you what do you reckon Lenny?'

'Na, they want him how he was when Lucy had him, an' that was before the rallying.'

'Yes that's right they want you like new Gari.'

'Did they ever get you fixed after that rallying then, Gari?'

'Yes. Fiona started driving me in rallies but she soon gave up so she could go abroad with George.

But when Fiona had done all her rallying I was sent to the work shop to have all the rally stuff removed and the original seats replaced and all the other things put back how they were. I was to say goodbye to rallying and although I was very sad to be sold again and a bit worried about who was going to be my next owner, I was not really sad at giving up all that fast driving.

After all I was 10 years old by this time and beginning to feel my age. The time I had spent with George and Fiona had gone very quickly, it didn't seem like eight years, but there is an old saying about time flying when you are having fun.

I stood for a while on a garage forecourt with a 'FOR SALE' sign on my roof, I was not in the showroom this time but outside in the wind and rain. I had a price sticker stuck to my windscreen and I stood there for some weeks.

Nobody, it seemed wanted to buy me I think the price they were asking for me was too high because after a few weeks the salesman came and scraped off the price ticket and stuck on another one.

Every Saturday a lad on a motorbike came round to the garage and stood there, staring at me for a few minutes, then he would get on his bike and ride away. Meanwhile I had fallen in love.'

'In love? wow, Gari pal, who was the lucky gal then?'

'Her name was Monica, she was a mini, not a Cooper and not a Morris, but an Austin, white with lovely red seats. I thought she was the most beautiful thing I had ever seen. At first she was over the other side of the forecourt and I used to just stare at her. She would look at me then look away and talk to the car next to her.

Quite soon we were all shifted about and we found that we were standing next to each other. I was very shy at first, funny because I never had trouble talking before but for some reason I became quite tongue tied. I wanted to tell her how I felt about her but I couldn't get the words out. Every day we would stand there chatting away about the weather and the people we could see walking down the street, the salesman, the other cars, but I still couldn't say the words to her that I wanted to say.

One day I couldn't stand it any longer and I shouted out to her, 'I love you'.

The salesman came out of the office when he heard my horn and said to the mechanic that I must have an electrical fault, he had better get me in and have a look.

But then Monica answered me. I heard her horn say 'I love you Gari'.

The salesman nearly fell over in surprise and said to the mechanic that it must be catching.

He said that the mechanic had better get the white one in as well and check the electrics on us both.

We spent the night in the workshop, and we stayed up the whole night, talking. After that if we ever found that we were not together on the forecourt we would talk to each other and would spend the night in the workshop.

Then one awful day someone came along and bought my Monica. For the second time in my whole life I felt so sad, I didn't want to talk to anyone or do anything. I stood there and stared down the road, hoping to catch a glimpse of her. I saw loads of white minis going up and down the road, and each time I stared so hard that I got some funny looks but I never saw my Monica again. I wonder to this day what happened to her, I hope she didn't end up in the crusher.'

STEVIE BOY

'How are you getting on with the body work then Jon?' Marc asked as he walked into the barn carrying a plate of sandwiches.

'Got about as far as I can for now, and then the shell is ready for the paint shop. Those for me?'

'They were, but I ate most of them coming across the yard, and then Rocky had one of course.'

'Ruth should teach that horse of hers some manners, what did he eat?'

'Only a ham and mustard one, I thought horses were not supposed to eat meat but that old fool will eat anything.'

'What's happening with all the mechanical bits then? This car will need an engine soon.'

'I checked the cam shaft and that seemed to be okay which is surprising considering how many miles it's done.

The valve gear also looks to be alright, the pistons have all been replaced, and all is ready for the new cylinder head.'

I am waiting for some more parts to come.'

'Right, Dad has sent off an order for new headlight bodies and indicators for the front, the rear ones are fine. He has also sent for some new wheels and all the other little bits like window catches, badges and I believe a new interior rear view mirror.'

Ruth rushed in at this point and asked in a rather desperate voice 'Has anybody seen Rocky lately?'

'He was in the yard a few minutes ago; he ate one of Jon's sandwiches, right off the plate.'

'Oh damn, the orchard gate is open, I bet he has found his way in there, can you come and help me get him, you know what he is like when he is let loose on those windfalls.'

All three ran out to rescue the horse from the orchard, or rather rescue the orchard from the horse.

Trevor had a good chuckle watching them go.

'He's a bit of a lad, on the quiet, that old horse' he told Gari.

'I haven't seen him, what is he like?'

'You will, he's a nosey ole horse, Ruth has had him a good long while, use to do a lot of jumping an that sort o thing but he be a bit old now so she don't ride him much, he is more like a pet sort of thing now a days an he do wander around the yard and get in the way. He's bound to come in an give you a looking over sooner or later, If he has been in the orchard for long he may get a tummy ache from all those apples, you ever had anything to do with horses then?'

'No, not really, I have seen them from a distance but never close up, I did have one owner who liked to bet on the races but we didn't often go to them, just to the betting shop.'

'How long were you in that there garage then?'

'Two months in all, but after Monica left it seemed more like five years. I was bought by the lad on the motor bike; he came by one day on foot, and really looked me over, under my bonnet, in my boot, right underneath me, in fact all over. He and the salesman took me out for a drive and when we got back there was a lady waiting there for us.
Stephen's Mum, Mrs Thain.

A few days later they arrived in a Jaguar and after a short time in the office Stephen came out with my keys in his hand. He looked as pleased as punch and he gave his mum a great big hug and said 'Thanks Mum you are the best.' She said that it was worth it to see him on four wheels instead of two.

'Off you go then and do try to drive carefully.'

Stephen laughed and got in; he started me up and revved up my engine. He slipped my clutch and we roared off down the road. I saw Mrs Thain shake her head as we zoomed past her. No wonder she wanted two extra wheels under him. If I had held any fond hopes of retiring from rallying I soon gave them up, but this rallying was not going to be of the official kind. This lad was going to drive everywhere at top speed.

I soon found that the old thrills were coming back, he drove very much like George and Fiona but not with such care, in fact he was a reckless driver and we got very close to other cars. I had a frightening time with this young man and I had the feeling that there were many more to come.

We went out of the town towards a small village, Stock, it was called, and there were some very bendy roads around that way. We just rounded one bend when I felt the indicator go on to the left. There was a large white gate which we just stopped in front of, and I mean just, with inches to spare.

Stephen got out and opened the gate, and then he drove me up a long winding drive. It was a gravel drive and there were stones flying out behind us in all directions, when we stopped in front of the house, more stones flew up and pinged off the walls and even the windows. A man came out of the house.

'If you are going to drive like a maniac you won't have that car for much longer.'

'Sorry Dad, I won't do that again, going too fast, I even scared myself then.'

'Your mother didn't help you buy that car just so that you could kill yourself in greater comfort, she, and I were hoping for some spark of responsibility to creep in there.'

'Don't nag Dad I said I wouldn't do it again, anyway what do you think of the car then?'

'Looks alright, good value was it? I hope your Mother didn't pay too much for it, not that I know much about the value of second hand cars.'

'Don't worry, I'm going to pay Mum back just as soon as I can and I won't ask you for a thing.'

'I suppose you are going to go flying off all over the countryside taking those artistic photographs of yours, I don't know why you can't get a proper job.'

'Not all this again, I don't want to be an accountant, I am a photographer and I can earn my living doing that.'

'There is nothing wrong with accountancy it has given us a good living, you have had nothing to complain about, ah here comes your Mother.'

'You two are not arguing again are you? I do wish you would learn to tolerate each other,' said Mrs Thain as she got out of the Jaguar.

'No we are not arguing, we have just finished, and I'm going to see Trish.'

With that Stephen jumped into my cab and slammed my door, we then roared out of the driveway and turned right onto the road, nearly hitting a man on a bike.

We drove down the road and very soon came to another large house. A girl of about 19 years came out. Stephen got out and went to her and hugged and kissed her. She broke away and looked at him.

'Another row with your Father?'

'How did you guess?'

We went back to Stephen's house and I waited outside while he and Trish went in to collect his camera. Then we went out even further into the countryside and I was parked near the top of a hill. I stood there while he took photos of Trish; she wanted to be a model and he was taking the photos for her portfolio. Much later we went back to Trish's house.

'I must go in and get my beauty sleep if I am ever to be a top model,' said Trish.

'Yes, you do that I am relying on you becoming famous because I will be your exclusive photographer, then we will both be rich and famous. That will show my father that there is more to life than books full of figures.'

Life with Stephen was very pleasant apart from his driving, but in time even that calmed down.

We went to some beautiful parts of the country and also some dirty places, some industrial estates and housing estates, and then there was the countryside, moor land and woodland. Seaside and riverside, we went all over so that he could take pictures.

Sometimes he would take a commission to photograph a certain area or thing, and very often on a Saturday there would be a wedding, I loved those. The bride always looked so pretty and I met some very nice cars, you may think that those big posh wedding cars were somewhat snobbish but as a lot of them were hire cars as such, they were all very nice to me.

One Saturday I was waiting with a Rolls Royce who was not a hire car but privately owned. We were having a nice chat when I saw Stephen coming towards us, deep in conversation with a smart looking man who took a package from my new friend.

'Okay then Stevie boy, you just take this little parcel to this address and I will see you right.' Stephen, I thought looked a bit nervous but he took the package and hid it under my driver's seat.

That evening we went for a long drive, we ended up in a deserted factory yard, Stephen stopped me and waited. Soon, ahead of us I saw the flash of a car's headlights.

Stephen retrieved the package from under my seat and went to meet a man.

He came back, got in me and we drove away very fast. The next day I saw my friend again, we went to meet him and his driver.

'Delivery made Stevie boy?'

Stephen told him there were no problems.

'Good, good, here is what I owe you and a little something extra for being a good boy.' He handed Stephen an envelope and a small package, they shook hands and we left.

When we arrived at Trish's house Stephen started to smoke something and the inside of my cab got all smoky and smelled strange.

People had smoked cigarettes in me before but this didn't smell like an ordinary cigarette, Stephen began to act strange.

Trisha and Stephen seemed to be very happy that night, Trish had received a letter that day saying that the modelling agency had accepted her and would have an assignment for her very soon, they also wanted Stephen to take the pictures. It was a celebration, at a restaurant.

Over the next few weeks we went to the meeting place often and then the next day I would see my friend. We also went into the town so that Trish and Stephen could go to the clothes shops; they became very smart with all
the most fashionable gear to wear.

Stephen bought some fancy lights for me, and some wide wheels and all sorts of bits and pieces. It became a sort of private joke between me and my Rolls Royce friend because whenever we met I would have some new part on me. The only thing I didn't like about all this time was the lingering smell in my cab of the funny cigarettes that Stephen and Trish were using.

One day when Stephen had made his delivery and was collecting his payment, the man said, 'Here's the cash and your present. Try these and see what you think Stevie boy.'

'Fair enough,' he yelled at her and drove me off fast. We went to see 'The Man'. He gave Stephen another package to deliver. Stephen told him he thought he had gone as far as he could with his paintings and was there something else he could take to give him an extra boost? The Man said he would get him something.

'What are they?'

'Just some little pills to pep you up a bit, all part of the rich tapestry of life, Stevie boy.' He patted Stephen on the arm, got into his car and drove away.

Stephen took one of the pills and wandered off on foot; he was a long time but eventually came back. This happened quite often and

Trish was worried about him. He was always tired when he got back and would tell Trish of all the weird dreams he had, but he said they were not dreams because he was awake. Hallucinations, he called them. Some were frightening and some were really nice and full of music and colour.

'I wish you would stop taking those things, they are changing you, and not for the better,' she said.

'You're wrong, I have found myself, I know where I am at now.'

He started painting on our trips out and left his camera at home. He was taking more and more of those tablets and I seemed to spend a lot of time on hill tops, in gate ways, and on country roads waiting for him. He always acted strange when he came back and his, already not wonderful driving, became much worse,

'What's happened to you Stephen? Trish asked him one day. You were going to be a famous photographer, you used to take really good pictures, now all you produce are these awful paintings, I don't think I want to see you anymore, not while you are still on those drugs.'

The new drugs had to be taken in a different way, Stephen was to inject them into his arm, they were expensive The Man said so if Stephen wanted anymore he would have to do some extra deliveries and he wouldn't get so much money.'

Gari stopped his story at this point; he heard a noise outside the barn.

WHO NEEDS THEM

Rocky peeped round the door, saw that there was something different in the barn and came in to have a sniff around. He was closely followed by Ruth who came in quietly, took hold of his head collar and led him out and back into his stable. Marc came in to fetch a screwdriver and a bag of screws.

'He has been picking his lock again,' he laughed to Jon.

'We should take him to the bank if he can break out of his stable so easily it should be a piece of cake for him to break into the bank vault.'

'He wouldn't leave any fingerprints anyway,' replied Jon.

'Well I can't do anymore to you Gari, you are going to be painted soon and then we are on the downhill run.' Jon picked up his empty plate as Rocky had eaten his sandwiches, and left the barn.

'There you go, pretty soon you going be looking like a real car again, what do you reckon to that then?'

'Mmm it sounds marvellous to me Trevor I would love to be out on the road again, I feel so fit and well.'

'Talk about fit and well, this here lad of yours do sound as if he be heading for some illness or other.'

'Ya he sounds a bit silly to me this boy.' Boris and Lenny were in the barn by this time.

'What come of him then pal?' asked Lenny.

'It's a very sad story, Lenny. Stephen started to shoot this stuff into his arms and it made him feel good. He let his hair grow and also grew a beard.

We didn't see much of his friends I often heard him say 'Who needs them'.

He stopped painting his weird pictures and got his camera out again. We were back to touring the countryside taking pictures and I thought that everything was back to normal except that he was more and more on his own and we started to go to a pub. Here he met with some new friends. Stephen would find that the nice feeling would wear off and then he would take another shot to make him feel good again. Each time he did it the feeling lasted for a shorter time and when it wore off he felt really ill. The stuff was expensive and soon he started selling all those nice clothes that he and Trish had bought, then all the extra bits that he had put on me, came off and were sold. Next was his camera.

There was nothing left to sell and one day he realised that he had to get some more money to buy the stuff, he went to see The Man.

'Can you get me some more deliveries? I need the money; I got to get some more stuff.' he asked.

'No can do Stevie boy but I will tell you how you can earn loads of money. What you do is buy a big load from me and then sell it on to your friends, build yourself up a round of customers like, see what I mean?'

'Become a pusher then!'

'Pusher, now that is a nasty word to use, I prefer to think of it as dealing.'

'Okay, but can you let me have some up front? I haven't got any money to buy it with.'

'Now you are getting into the realms of fantasy, you come up with the money and I will get you the goods.'

'But I need some now, and how am I supposed to get the money?'

'That's not my problem Stevie boy, come and see me when you have the cash.'

The Man got into his car and drove away, Stephen stood for a long time, he began to shiver and as I waited for him I saw that he was not looking very well. His skin was very pale; all round his eyes were dark rings as if he had been punched. I also saw that he was getting very thin and didn't stand up straight anymore but he was hunched over. He was always cold and whenever we drove around he would have my heater going full blast.

The driving was worse than ever, we would often hit a kerb when going round corners, and even on straight roads Stephen didn't seem to be able to keep me in a straight line. Somehow he got us home. Mrs Thain was cutting some flowers and came over to us when we arrived.

'Stephen, you look dreadful' she cried.

'Mum can you let me have some money there is something I have got to buy.'

'I think I know what is wrong with you, no, I cannot give you money for drugs.'

Stephen shrugged and sort of shuffled indoors. He looked as if walking was painful to him.

Soon Stephen appeared again and he was holding Mrs Thain's handbag, he got in me and we drove down the driveway. I saw his mother standing on the doorstep watching us go, she was crying.

Once we were out on the road Stephen stopped me and I could feel him tip the contents of the bag onto my passenger seat. He gave a grunt as he counted the cash in her purse, then we went to see The Man again.

'That won't buy you very much will it Stevie Boy, still I will let you have a little to keep you going, here you go. Stay lucky' The Man walked away laughing.

Stephen lost no time in shooting some of this stuff into his arm, by now he always had all the things he needed to do it nearby, he kept them in a box under my driver's seat.

'That's good', he sighed.

'Now I must get some more money.' he knew where he could get it.

Each time we left the house Stephen would drive me to a shop in the town. The first time we went there he sat for a long time before he went in and as he walked round me I saw he had a gold chain in his hand. I had seen it, this chain, it belonged to his mother.

When he came out of the shop he had some money and again we went to see The Man. He asked The Man once more for some more delivery jobs so that he could get some money together but The Man said, 'Sorry Stevie Boy, I can't use you, I mean look at the state of you, you're a wreck. I don't think I can go on supplying you, in fact you are becoming a liability.'

'You can't stop selling to me, please, what am I going do without a supply?'

'Come up with some big money then Stevie Boy.'

As he drove me along the road he kept saying to himself 'Big Money, Big Money, got to get Big Money, but where?'

We were going along far too fast, Stephen was not paying much attention, I could see that we were approaching a set of traffic lights. They were on red but Stephen didn't slow me down he just carried on. I tried to slow down for him but he had his foot firmly pressed on my accelerator and still we kept going towards the red light.

The worst happened; we went straight through the red light and as we were going across the junction a car came on to us from the left.

He swerved to try and get around us but there was not enough room or time and he crashed into my back wing, I spun round and hit a bollard with my other back wing.

My engine stalled and we just stood there for a while, Stephen was very still.

Soon I heard sirens, and saw police cars and an ambulance. The police started asking people what happened and if they had seen the accident. The other car driver was pretty shook up but no hurt at all, which was very lucky for him, but Stephen was still not moving. After what seemed like ages they got Stephen out of me and put him in the ambulance and drove away.

Then a breakdown vehicle picked up my rear end and towed me to a garage.

THE JOB

Trevor chugged into the yard with the trailer and stopped by the door of the barn.

'I've got all the wood and stuff' called Jon, 'probably best to leave it on the trailer for now isn't it Dad?'

Nick was in the barn studying the far corner. The barn was a tall building but there was an upper floor at that end, where the hay was stored.

'This is the best place to build it, under the low ceiling. If we put it in the corner there will be two outside walls for extractor fans to clear the fumes.'

Gari glanced at Trevor, as if to ask what was going on but Trevor just shrugged, he didn't know.

Nick, Jon and Marc got to work. First they cleared the space and then they set to building a room in the corner with all the wood that Trevor had brought. It took them two days of hard work to get the structure in place, they put fans into the outside walls, they painted the concrete floor with rubberised paint and then most puzzling of all they lined the whole structure with big plastic sheets.

It was all very strange and Gari was dying to find out what it was for.

'This looks like a very permanent and expensive piece of building for one car, does this mean that you are going to make a regular hobby of doing them up?' Lucy asked when she came to have a look at all their work.

'The first of many, my dear, just the first of many,' Nick told her.

'That's what they do call a spray booth, It's where they is going put you to do your painting, see as got to be kept clean and hot so your paint do dry right.' Trevor told him.

'How are they going to get me in there, I am still standing on these axle stands?'

'Don't know about that boy, some new bits have come I think Marc did say they was sub frames, or something like that.'

'Oh then I can have my wheels back on.'

Boris and Lenny came in that night, there was still room for them but things were a bit cramped now and Boris became very nervous that he might get a scratch.

'So this one small car is the cause of much discomfort for all of us' he said grumpily.

'If my paintwork becomes damaged I will hold you responsible for it, Gari Cooper.'

'Don't be such a grouch, I for one think its quite cosy in here now, and there's space for us all, plenty of room still,' Gari answered

'That's right Pal,' Lenny said. 'Now tell us about this poor lad of yours, did you see him again?'

'No, I never saw him again. After he came out of hospital, because he had broken some bones he had to go to prison, because the police had found some of the drugs and stuff under my seat. He had also been banned from driving for a year, because he had been driving while he was under the influence of the drugs, and he had to pay a big fine for not stopping at the red light.

I was to be sold again, to Trish. She came to see me and brought a man with a low loader. They winched me up and took me to a garage to be repaired, again.

Quite a lot of work this time and because Stephen had not paid his insurance she had to pay for it to be done. But by the time they had finished with me I looked really smart again.

Trish came and picked me up a few days later and we drove to London. She lived here most of the time, sharing a house with three other girls.

One day I was waiting for Trish to come out of the shop, she was buying a new dress I think. She had parked me in a space by a meter and the money was running out so I hoped she wouldn't be long.

I felt someone open my door lock, it was not Trish it was a man, and he had a key. I was just wondering how he had got that when he got in and started my engine.

He carefully pulled out into the stream of traffic and drove me away but didn't go very fast, just carefully.

I didn't know where we were going, and where Trish was. We drove for a few miles and came to a part of London that I had never seen before. We drove alongside a railway line for a while, then the road went down a hill and the track carried straight on over a kind of bridge which was made up from arches.

The road curved round and I saw that we were under the bridge and all the arches had doors on them. We stopped outside the third one along and the man sounded my horn. The big double doors in front of me opened and the man drove me in. There were two other cars in there, a Granada which was dark blue and another mini.

Two men came over to me and started to take off my number plates. I couldn't imagine why they should want to do this but I recognised one of them. I had seen him at the garage that Trish took me to for my MOT test and service. He was the mechanic, I remembered him because he was chatting to Trish for quite a long time and she had gone all giggly and had driven over the kerb when we left. I still wondered just what I was doing here.

'This one will be fine I serviced it last week.'

'Okay, but check it over anyway we don't want anything conking out on us, you finished with that Granada? We got to get them all ready for Friday.'

'All finished' the mechanic said putting the bonnet down on the Granada.

'And that's false plates on all of them now, the Minis are ready to park up on Thursday night.'

The Mini said his name was Michael and he was a family car, his owner had a couple of kids who left all their sweet wrappers on his back seat.

He used to get annoyed about it but he said he wished he was with then now and would never moan again about the untidy kids.

As soon as the men had gone I asked the other cars if they knew what was happening. The Granada who introduced himself as

Graham said that we had been stolen and were to be used in a 'Job'.

'These men are bank robbers and we are to be used as their getaway cars,' said Graham.

'What happens to us afterwards?' Michael asked, by this time I was too scared to ask questions.

'We get dumped,' was the reply.

'Will we ever be found again?'

'Of course we will' Graham said reassuringly but I could feel that he was worried.

The men didn't come back for some time and without the lights on it was difficult to tell if it was night or day.

Then they came, the men. We noticed it was quite dark, when they opened the big double doors. There were two of them this time, the mechanic got into Michael and the other one drove me out. He left my engine running while he got out closing the doors

and then we followed Michael back up the way I had come
in. After a while the two men stopped us in a car park, or it looked like a car park, there were certainly lines drawn for cars to stop in but it was not very big.

They parked us back to back so that each was pointing towards one of the two entrances. I could see from the way the lines were drawn that we would be able to drive directly out of the place and we should not get blocked in.

There we waited getting more and more tense as the time passed, all that night and a good part of the next day as well, then we heard, rather than saw, Graham as he squealed into the car park and stopped very close to us.

The men tumbled out of him and ran to us, we had been left unlocked so they got in and started us up. Michael went first; I called 'Bye Michael'. I was driven away at top speed, I just heard Graham breathe with a deep sigh 'Bye Boys'.

That was when I heard the police cars. They were chasing us. Here we go I thought, just pretend you are on a special stage. We turned right, out of the car park across the traffic in front of some cars who blasted their horns at us. Then when the horns didn't stop I realised just how close the police were to us.

I knew these men had done something bad but I began to get caught up in the excitement of the moment. Anyway the next turn we made was a left turn that was not so bad because even though we were going very fast I was fairly certain that we were not going to hit anything. The police car was very close and now he was joined by another one.

We were on a big road, very wide and there was not much traffic so even though I was going at my top speed the police were gaining on us.

My driver realised that if he was to lose them we would need to get into smaller roads where I could get around better than the big powerful police cars. So we turned left at the next junction. This led to an industrial estate with lots of small roads, with factories, garages and such like in each one.

The very first factory we came to had a large gate, out of which was coming a big lorry. Luckily the driver saw us and stopped, leaving us room to get around him, and the police cars followed. My driver swore and drove on as fast as he could and suddenly turned another corner this time to the right. The first police car was so close that he didn't have time to turn and went straight on, but the second one followed us round. There was a skip parked in the road and a man pushing a wheel barrow was crossing to it.

By going up on to the path we just managed to get past him, but it slowed down the car behind us, because the man with the barrow had to scramble out of his way. My driver grunted his satisfaction at this and turned another corner. This time the road was clear and we made good speed but as we rounded a bend we saw that it was a dead end. The only thing to do was take the very next corner we came to which was to the right.

We skidded around that corner and with my tail end waving about like mad we accelerated along this road until another lorry began to emerge from yet another gateway. This one was not so quick to see us and carried on coming out.

The bank robber sounded my horn but did not slow down, there was still just room for us to get through, but the gap was closing. The driver of the lorry had not seen or heard us and was still coming. We shot through the gap and nearly made it, but the lorry caught my back wing and swung me round so we were once again facing the lorry. The damage was not too bad and did not hinder me, but 'Oh' did it hurt.

My driver then shoved my gears into reverse and did a very neat backwards handbrake turn, by the time we were facing the other way he already had me in forward gear and away we went again. The lorry was by this time reversing so that the police car could get through, who came after us fast with his siren blaring.

That was when my driver made a dreadful mistake, he decided that he should take the next left turn; this took us into a much smaller road, very narrow with no room to turn quickly. We had just about straightened into this road when we saw the other police car pull out of a side road and completely block our path. Behind us the chasing car had just turned into the road, we were blocked in, there was no escape we were trapped.

The men fell out of my cab and started running. I just stood there, cooling down. One of the police cars said 'You did well there, but you just didn't have the power to get away from us.'

I asked what would happen now and he told me not to worry I would be able to have a nice rest. In fact I rested there for most of the day.

A man came to me carrying a big black bag, which looked a bit like a doctor's bag. He took a soft brush from the bag and a pot of powder, which he dusted all over my steering wheel, the door handles, dash board and various other parts of me. He then took a camera and shot off lots of photographs, close to the powdered bits and from far away.

He said to one of the policemen that he had to show how I had come to rest. When he had finally finished with all the powder a flat bed trailer arrived. I was then driven onto the trailer and lashed down, then we made our rather bumpy way to a place called the Car Pound.

This was attached to the Police Station and it was here that, when I was safely back on the ground, the man appeared and began to strip me down. Of course this had happened before, when they were searching for Stephen's drugs, so I knew what was going on. The bag that had all the money in it was not inside my cab, Michael had taken that. But they did find some gloves and balaclava masks which belonged to the robbers, and that was about all, so they put me back together and took me to another part of the compound to park me up. There were Graham and Michael waiting for me.

'Oh, you are hurt' cried Michael 'how did it happen?'

So I told him all that had happened since I left the car park, then I asked about their experience.

Michael sighed and said that he didn't even get out of the car park, as he drove to the exit about three police cars turned into it and surrounded him so that he couldn't move.

'Now that you are here Graham will tell us his story, he wouldn't tell me he said he only wanted to tell it once.'

'Hreumph!' began Graham, 'Well in the morning after you left, all the men came to the arches, they all got into my cab and leaving the doors of the garage open we sped to town. When we arrived at the bank, the driver stayed with me and the other three went in. they were in longer than the driver expected, I could tell he was becoming concerned because he kept revving my engine and was riding on my clutch.

At last they came running out and jumped into my seats and even before they had got the doors closed the driver was off. A car pulled out behind us and I noticed that it was a police car, they had been waiting for us to go and they obviously knew why we were there, the men were very angry and there was a lot of shouting and swearing going on in my cab as we tried to getaway. It was quite a chase to the car park where you two were waiting, and the rest you know.'

IN ENGLAND NOW

Putting Gari's new sub frames into his body shell proved to be much easier than taking the old ones out had been. Once that was done Jon could get on with the job he had not been able to do on Gari's sills.

He repaired all the rusty patches on the inner sills and welded on new outer sills and then he found he could weld on new front wings. Marc jacked Gari up and put his wheels on, that meant he could than change all the break pipes and handbrake cable. Then all three men pushed Gari backwards into the new room.

This was not easy because they had not yet put his steering column back into place. But with a lot of pushing and pulling they placed him in the centre of the remaining floor space, beside the tables. They then carried the new doors, bonnet and boot lid and laid them on the tables.

Once he was in place Marc again removed the wheels and placed Gari back onto the axle stands.

Then he set to work on the insides of Gari's wheels.

He put new brake drums and break shoes on each in turn and then he put the wheels into the back of Lenny,' he told Nick, 'I'll take those wheels to be grit blasted, and sprayed before we take them for their new tyres.'

'Okay then, Jon, what do you want me to do here?' asked Nick.

'First you grind off all the welds and get them nice and flat,' started Jon.

'Stop, that is enough to be going on with,' laughed Nick. 'I thought being a farmer was hard work.'

So when Nick next had some spare time he came into the room in the barn and began to grind at the welds. Gari found this rather painful but he didn't like to complain, after all he wanted to look his best. Later Jon came in and Nick proudly showed off his work but Jon just stood there and shook his head.

'Lots more to do yet Dad, it's not nearly flat enough.'

Nick shrugged his shoulders and said 'Oh well I will have another look tomorrow.'

Lenny came in with a strange looking machine, which Marc and Jon unloaded and lugged into the room.

'It's called a compressor,' he told Gari and went on to explain that it was to be used to put the paint on.

'Well there is a lot of rubbing down to do first,' giggled Gari.

'Better here than in the car pound then is it?'

'Much, it was really boring there, there were other cars to talk to but most of them only stayed for a day or two.'

'How was that then?'

'Well they were only there because their owners had parked them in the wrong place and the police had towed them away. Michael was very home sick, he said he even missed the sticky sweets and having the back of his seats kicked by the children. Graham was rather glad of his rest but after a while he was itching to get back on the road. We stood there for quite a few weeks. Trish eventually came along with a tall young policeman. She was talking and giggling and I wondered if we were going to drive over any kerbs on the way out.

The policeman was saying that there was some damage done to me but that the garage would soon get it fixed and the insurance would take care of it.

'I have to sell it anyway, I am going to work for one of the big fashion houses in Paris, and will need to buy a car in France.'

'Well the best of luck to you and drive carefully now.'

Trish drove straight over the kerb on her way out and we went directly to a car auction place.

The rest of the day went in a kind of blur, all of a sudden there were people everywhere, they were jumping in and out of cars, lifting bonnets here and opening boots there. They crawled underneath, kicked tyres and started engines. There was noise and exhaust fumes everywhere. We were all lined up and one by one we were driven closer to the building.'

When a person was interested in a car they would go inside and wait for it to come through so that he could make his bid. The noise inside was tremendous, car engines revving, people shouting and above all this noise was the sound of the auctioneer. What he did was to say a price and the people in the crowd would raise their hands or something if they were willing to pay that figure, then he would raise the price and the people stopped raising their hands, the last person to do so would be the new owner.

When it was my turn the auctioneer said, 'Well. Ladies and Gentlemen, here we have a nice little Mini Cooper S, with an unusual number plate which alone is worth a pretty penny. Good little runner, bit of a history but nothing that should detract from the best price, a car of character what am I bid for this motor?

Make me an offer now, how about...?'

I stopped listening at this point and began to look around at the people, wondering which one, if any, would be my next owner. I flushed up with pride when I saw loads of hands and eventually it was between two people.

One was a weird looking man, he stood there apparently reading a book, and sticking up his hand whenever he heard the auctioneer's voice boom out.

He was short and stout; he wore a very old battered tweed hat that did its best to cover a great shock of frizzy white hair which stuck out in all directions. He had on a cape that was originally black but this was very old and threads were hanging from. Under that I could see a shirt that must have been white once upon a time but now it was a pale grey colour, and a big red spotted bow tie was crocked and hanging from his neck. Over this was a pink jumper that looked about two sizes too small for him because it did not quite meet the top of his trousers, it stretched over his rotund belly and the checked trousers, which were mainly green, hung down under it. These were held in place by a pair of paisley pattern braces and a big leather belt. I stole a glance at his feet, he had thick woollen socks and, would you believe, sandals.

He was a very strange sight and the pipe that was hanging from his teeth was adding to the general smell of the auction ring. Actually the smell of the smoke was rather pleasant in comparison with the exhaust fumes.

'Down to you Sir, Mr?'

'Oh yes-er-yes-um Professor Cargill, at your service Sir.'

The old man said digging into his pocket and walking towards the auctioneers stand.

'Right Sir, if you take this ticket round to the office they will give you the keys so you can take the car for a test drive.'

'Yes-er-um thank you, very kind very kind' and he shuffled off mumbling.

'Test drive, hum got to take it for a test drive yes I suppose I must hum' he was mumbling as he approached.

He got in and started me up, and when he finally found the gear he wanted we shot forward and left the compound, we were out for about ten minutes but he had taken the words 'Test Drive' very seriously indeed. He thrashed me, making my engine race between changing gear and threw me round corners left and right. By the time we got back to the compound I was a nervous wreck. He got out and shuffled back to the office. I could see him from where I was, and noticed that he took money from each pocket and handed it over to the cashier.

Now he was not on a test drive he drove me away in a very sedate manner, in fact apart from veering over to the wrong side of the road every now and again it was a nice gentle ride. When he did go over to the right, I heard him say to himself 'In England now' and he would pull over to the left again.

We drove along for quite a while and I knew I was getting short of petrol.

The Prof didn't seem to notice this because we passed lots of petrol stations on our way and he never showed any signs of slowing down, let alone stopping. He drove as if he had something on his mind but I was soon to realise that he was often like this. Of course the inevitable happened, I ran out of fuel, way out in the country miles away from anywhere. I chugged to a standstill and the Prof sat there for a while silent.

I was beginning to think that there was something wrong with him when he at last got out of me and muttering as he went, he wandered back down the road.

It was dark by the time he found me again, he poured a gallon of petrol into me from a can he was carrying and getting in he tried to start me. It took a few goes before the fuel got through and then we were away in a big 'U' turn I supposed to take the can back to the garage. We had gone down the road about half a mile when he stopped me and muttered 'Oh dear will I ever get home?'

We turned round again and when we got back to where I ran out of fuel I could see why, he had left the petrol can in the middle of the road.

Well life with this one was certainly going to be interesting.

It was very late by the time we arrived at a small cottage which was set in the grounds of a big house. The Prof got out of me but he left the keys in my ignition and the lights were still on.

When morning came I could have a look around at my new home, this cottage was one of three set close together and near a big gate. I could see a sign by the gate but I couldn't read the words. There was another car parked outside the next door cottage and to him I said in a very quiet voice 'Good morning'.

'I expect you are a bit low what with having your lights on all night, your Professor is a bit absent minded, but then so in a way is mine.'

'Yours is a Professor as well then?' I asked.

'Yup, my name is Ian the Hillman Imp and the place you have found yourself in is a college in the famous University City of Cambridge.'

'You sound very proud to be here, is it a nice place to live?'

'Not bad at all, and we don't have to do much work, well I don't anyway, mine doesn't go very far, you may have to though.'

'They are both Professors you say, does that mean they teach?'

'Oh yes, mine is the History Professor and yours is the head of the Archaeology Department,' Ian told me.

'Excuse me, the what? Department?'

'Archaeology, don't you know what that is? Your Prof dashes about all over the country digging up old bones and bits of pottery, he and my Professor have some terrific rows sometimes because the teachings of mine do not always relate to the findings of yours. You will hear them sometime.'

'Why, do they argue in public then?'

'Sometimes; but more often, they are indoors and they can still be heard from out here. It gets to be quite a joke with the students; they come and listen to them. Oh here we go yours is about to find out about your lights.'

I looked over to the front door of the cottage to see my Prof emerging. He was not wearing his cloak and hat. I could see now that his head on the top was smooth and shiny with not a single hair. He came over to me and looked into my cab.

'Keys, how did they get in there, tut tut.'

He got in and tried to start me but my battery was so flat that all I could manage was a small cough.

'Hmm left your lights on did I? Silly me.'

Some students came by, 'Nice car Professor Cargill'.

'Hmm yes but I seem to have left the lights on all night and now the poor little thing cannot start.'

'Hop in and we'll give you a push Prof, we will bump start it.'

And so began my first day at University.

ONLY ONCE A WEEK

Nick had another try at getting Gari's welds nice and flat, finally, when his arms were aching fit to drop off Jon pronounced that he was satisfied with his father's work. Now that all the spaces between the welds could be seen they were able to fill them, and then came more rubbing down. Gari found that this did not hurt nearly so much. What he did find strange was the feeling in his wheel arches, Jon was spraying on some weird stuff which was lumpy. This was called stone chip and it was designed to stop the stones flying up into the wheel arches and chipping the paintwork.

'That's fine Dad, now we can put the stopper on.'

'What does the stopper do then?'

'Shows up any bad bits.'

So on went the stopper, and then that had to be rubbed down.

But now that Nick was using the fine paper it did not hurt, in fact it was quite pleasant. As soon as Nick had finished Jon was to spray primer on all the welds, just to make sure they were all flat.

Of course they wouldn't be flat, Jon could see some lumps and holes, so on went some more stopper.

'That's enough for today, my arms are aching and I still have the milking to do,' Nick said.

'Okay I'll spray another coat of primer on and we can see if it's flat enough.'

'What then?'

'More rubbing down.'

'Oh boy,' Nick muttered as he wandered out of the barn 'I am beginning to wonder if this was such a good idea.'

Jon laughed and shook his head as he started up the compressor.

Poor Nick, he never thought that there was so much rubbing involved in the painting of a car, but eventually he got it done well enough to pass Jon's critical inspection and they began to spray on the primer.

This took away Gari's patchwork look and he was a fetching shade of grey all over. For Gari this was the worst so far, Jon and Nick wore masks which filtered out the worst of the smells but poor Gari had to stand there without even his front grille for protection. The fumes from the paint made him feel very sick and dizzy.

Jon looked him over very carefully and then went to start up the compressor again. Gari found all this very difficult to cope with, on the one hand he hated the spraying with all his might and he also hated the way it made him feel so ill but on the other hand he was grateful to Jon, and the rest of the family for giving him a chance to be smart again, it was all very confusing.

When Jon at last opened the doors of the spray booth and the air cleared slightly Gari was feeling much better, he knew he was nearly half way through the spraying operation and in a few days it would all be over. Jon and Nick left Gari in the small room with the heating on full so that his new paint would dry off quickly. Later when the other vehicles had been parked up in the barn Jon came to have a look at his work; he then turned off the heating lamps and left the door ajar.

'Feeling a bit bad are you pal?' asked Lenny.

'You look a bit pale,' he joked.

Gari giggled, he was still feeling a bit drunk from the paint fumes and the heat of the room but as the fresh air came in from outside the barn his mind began to clear.

'Phew! I got so dizzy and sick there I thought that I was going to fall off my axle stands. Have you ever been re-sprayed? If you haven't then think yourself lucky it is really awful.'

'I am too new for that and why would Lenny and Trevor need it?'

'I don't think I would be wanting it anyway, an I couldn't stand all that polishing an washing that you do get every blooming week, Boris,' said Trevor.

'Well I used to look smart but I reckon I'm more comfy as I am a scruff' said Lenny. 'You going to be same colour as you were then Gari?
Cream roof and green was it?'

'Yes the same, and factory fresh.'

'Are we to sit discussing your colour all of the night? I want to hear about this Prof.'

'Ah my Prof, well life with him was never dull, Angelina and Jamie his daughter and grandson came to stay for a while and she cleaned up the cottage.

'Dad, I have put an advert in the post office window for a cleaner and cook for you.'

'What an amazingly good idea, you are a clever girl.'

The lady Angelina found was perfect for the Prof, Mrs Green, she said she would pop in everyday through the week and cook a meal which Prof could eat when he came home, and she was quite prepared to clean around the books and papers. She said she would leave a list of food stuffs for the Prof to buy each week so that she had all she required to cook his meals. He was quite looking forward to going out shopping with his list. He decided that he would go on his way home from taking Angelina and Jamie to the station.

Of course our first visit to the supermarket was a disaster.

There were two big supermarkets near the station and they both had big car parks attached to them. We pulled out of the station and turning right we very soon came to the first of them. Here the Prof parked me up and for some reason he locked my doors, something he never remembered to do normally. The thing is he didn't park in the car park but outside the shop, where there was a waiting limit of one hour.

He went into the shop and seemed to be an awfully long time, well over the hour. When he came out he had no shopping with him and I wondered what had happened. You see he had forgotten to take any money with him, and he had lost his keys.

'Have to go home and get the spare, he muttered and wandered off in the direction of the bus stop. I saw him on a bus but was not sure it was going the right way.

The next thing I knew was that my front end was being lifted up. I knew where I was going, the Pound.'

'And wot happened to your Prof, did he ever find this out?'

'Yes he did find out, it was the talk of college. The Prof was, as I suspected, on the wrong bus and going in the wrong direction.

He saw a book shop and decided to have a browse.

While in the bookshop he decided he was hungry and so he went in search of food. That made him remember that he was supposed to be doing something but he had totally forgotten what it was, so he headed for a park that he had seen so that he could sit down and think about this. When he reached the park he sat down on the grass and watched the children play, then he lay down and let the sun shine on his face, very soon of course he was asleep.

So now we have the situation of my Prof asleep in the park in one town, me having by this time been towed to the pound, and the people in the supermarket waiting for him to come back and pay for the groceries. The manager had taken the trolley to his office.

Now the thing about the Prof is that when he falls asleep it takes an earthquake to wake him up, so when a football bounced right off his head without him stirring, you can imagine the reaction of the people there. One lady thought he was dead and fainted on the spot, another found that he had a pulse and still could not wake him so an ambulance was called. Well he didn't wake up as they put him onto a stretcher, he didn't wake up in the ambulance, and he didn't wake up when they got him to the hospital.

He did wake up a couple of hours later by which time he was dressed only in a hospital gown and was tucked up in bed.

Then he remembered what he was supposed to be doing and thought that he had better go and get on with his shopping. So he left the hospital, just like that, still dressed in this gown, he walked out of the building out of the grounds and down the road.

When he realised his state of dress he turned and headed back to the hospital, trying to keep out of sight. He did succeed in getting into the hospital but found himself in the maternity block. There he was surrounded by pregnant ladies and babies. A ward sister came to him and asked what he thought he was doing there.

'In all honesty, my dear I do not know what I am doing here, I thought I was asleep in the park.'

Eventually the Prof and his clothes reunited and he was sent on his way, the only trouble was he didn't know where on earth he was now, but luckily he bumped into Professor Drummond.

'What on earth are you doing in St. Neots old boy and why have you no money with you?'

My Prof told his story and by the time he had finished Professor Drummond was laughing so much that tears were streaming from his eyes.

'Of course I will reimburse you when we get home,' Prof Cargill ended.

'No, no old chap wouldn't hear of it.' laughed Professor Drummond.

'You have more than paid your fare in entertainment.'

When they got back to the cottages my Prof was apparently a little worried that the door would be locked, but Ian told me that Professor Drummond bet £5 that the door was open, and he won the bet. Mrs Green had left a casserole in the oven that the two professors shared for supper, with a bottle of wine.

They were just finishing the wine when there was a knock at the door, and upon opening it my Prof found that the caller was a Policeman.

'You are the owner of a green Mini Cooper, number GAR 1C sir?'

'Yes officer that is my car.'

'Here is the release paper for it sir, it is in the pound and there is a fine to pay before it can be released, if you come along tomorrow with the required amount you will be able to collect it. Thank-you Sir, goodnight.'

'Drummond, old man; have you any idea where the car pound might be?'

'None whatsoever, dear chap, but if you call a cab in the morning and ask them to take you there you will find out for future reference,' chuckled Drummond.

This is exactly what he did, and this time he brought lots of money with him, enough to pay the taxi, enough to pay for my release and even enough to pay for his shopping. When the Prof went back to the supermarket he found that his groceries were still waiting for him in the manager's office, so at last he was able to pay for them.

'Thank the Lord that I only have to come shopping once a week' he said as he settled into my driver's seat.'

UP POPPED THE FLAG

Nick didn't do any work on Gari for a couple of weeks. When he did come again into the little room there stood Gari, covered in a fine dust. Nick connected a hose to the outside tap and a fine rose to the business end. He turned on the water and gave Gari a nice cooling shower to wash off all the dust; he then rinsed the floor and the walls of the booth. He put on the heaters and closed the door.

After a while Gari was feeling very hot and a little uncomfortable, but soon Nick returned, opened the doors wide and turned off the heaters. He selected a fine paper and began the laborious task of once again rubbing down Gari's bodywork. Jon would be coming soon to spray on the first coat of green and Nick couldn't wait, after all this work he was dying to see the little car in his proper colours.

By the end of the day Gari had the first two coats of green.

Nick was to do a final rub down with the finest paper before the last coat was sprayed on.

There was only the cream roof to do and his paintwork would be finished. Then Gari would be able to come out of the little room and stand in the barn with his friends, they would not have as much space as they did before because the spray booth was to stay for the next car, which Nick already had his eye on.

'What sort of car is it Trevor? Have you heard?'

I did ear tell that it was another Mini like you boy, and they was going do it up for Ruth' answered Trevor.

'For everyday driving; not just for showing off like they do want you for.'

'Well having been through it I will be able to tell this car what to expect and if I forget anything you will be able to remind me.'

'Your memory can't be all that bad or do you think you've been affected by your Prof? He seems to have lost is brain, did he lose it or just misplace it?' joked Trevor.

'The Prof was terrible when he had nothing to occupy him but as soon as he had something to think about he was really clever. When he had conversations with Professor Drummond or some students on Archaeology he was so bright you would never think he was the same person. He never forgot anything he promised to do for Jamie or Angelina, after the first time that is, but he never seemed to be able to remember to do things for himself.

As for my lights, well my battery was more often flat than it was charged up and because he was always letting it go flat I needed new ones much more often than I should have. Before Jamie came up with his little devise that is.

Jamie was coming to stay on his own; the Prof was to meet his train at 10.30 in the morning. Angelina had phoned and told him the time to be at the station, there was only one problem, my lights, they had been on all night again and so my battery was absolutely dead. When the time came for the Prof to drive me to the station he tried my engine and then swore, which is something I didn't very often hear.

He went in a taxi.

'Jamie, just get into the car while I push it so that we can get it started, I am afraid I left the lights on as usual. If we get it started we can go for a drive in the country to charge up the battery again and then we can find a nice pub to go to for lunch. I don't believe I have any lectures to give this afternoon. You are old enough to go into a pub are you not? Of course you are, anyway you look old enough. Oh dear how am I ever going to remember to turn off the lights, I spend more time pushing this car than I do driving it.'

Jamie was thoughtful and then I noticed he took a piece of paper from his pocket and a pencil.

He made a list of things which he told his Grandfather he needed and asked if they could stop in the city on the way home.

'I hope you don't mind but there are some lectures I must give over the next couple of days but after that I am free for the rest of the week.'

'That's okay Granddad I have just given myself a project to do over the next couple of days, but I will need your car' Jamie held up his hand 'I know I can't drive it but I need it all the same, you will see why very soon, in a couple of days to be exact.'

So on our way home we went into the city, and I noticed that the Prof always parked in a car park these days and never on the side of the road. I was glad of that; I didn't really want to spend too much time in the pound, although I met some very nice vehicles there.

For the next couple of days Jamie spent most of his time inside the cottage but every now and again he would come out to me and look very closely under my dash board. Once he came out to me with a screwdriver and I got really worried. Then he pulled my ignition to bits and fitted some new parts into it. The last thing he did was to screw something onto my dashboard close to the middle. Then he spent some time putting in my ignition key and taking it out, each time making some kind of adjustment to the new items he had fitted.

'Here you are the Granddad; you will never leave the lights on again.'

The Prof sat in my driver's seat and began to laugh, what he was laughing at was a small flag which was standing up in the middle of the dash, on the flag was written 'lights'.

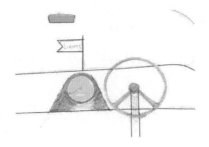

'Try the key,' said Jamie.

When the Prof inserted my ignition key the flag flopped down, when he removed the key the flag popped up with its message. The Prof clapped his hands and laughed out so loud that Professor Drummond popped his head out to see what was going on.

'Come Drummond, look at this that my Grandson has invented, it is marvellous, simply marvellous.'

Professor Drummond asked Jamie how it worked. Jamie explained that there was an electro-magnet which was turned on by the ignition and which held the flag down, when the ignition was switched off the magnet also went off and the flag, which was on a spring, popped up with the message.

'Oh dear boy you simply have to make me one, not that I ever leave my lights on but it is such fun that I must have one.'

'Ho ho you never leave your lights on Drummond, because you never drive in the dark.'

'That is totally beside the point Cargill.

'I would be glad to Professor Drummond,' Jamie said shyly.
After that my Prof managed to turn off my lights and I never again suffered from flat battery syndrome.'

'How is it that Jamie was there in the term time, He should've been at school?' Trevor asked.

'Well I think he had just taken his exams, 'O' levels I think they were called, so he was finished with school for the summer. He was to go back to school after the summer holidays to do the higher exams so that he could go to college, and study electronics.

But in the meantime he had to come to stay and then he and the Prof were going on a holiday together and they were taking me. I was not sure where we were going but I knew we were to start in Suffolk, where Jamie and his parents lived.

Angelina and Tom lived in a large house in the town of Southwold where they were both teachers. The Prof liked Southwold because it was a nice quiet town by the sea and there was a big green where the dog, Duke could run around for hours without getting in anyone's way. Duke was to stay with Angelina.

Naturally, on the way up to Southwold Jamie had to sit in the back seat along with the cases that would not fit in the boot because Duke was not going to give up his front seat for anyone.

When we arrived at Jamie's home Duke thought he liked the look of the beach and so Jamie took him for a run, he was feeling a bit cramped anyway he said.

The house was situated on the cliff top and as it was not a very high cliff, from where I was parked I could see Jamie and the dog. Duke had never been on the beach before and he had never seen the sea, I could see that he was puzzled by it. After all; the river in Cambridge did not have waves like this and it tasted different. I think he liked the waves, I saw him jumping in and out between them but he did not seem to like the taste of it very much.

We were going camping; it was quite a while since I was on a camping holiday. I wondered where we were going this time.

'My dear, you seem to have packed us enough food there to feed an army. Are you expecting the car to eat as well?'

Angelina came to me, she opened my door, lifted my driver's seat up and removed my back seat, I thought this brings back memories!

She then began to pack boxes into the space and bags as well. I don't have to explain it to you it had all happened before. She was packing me up for the holiday; she didn't trust any of the men folk in her life to do the job properly so she did it herself.

From what I could see of the equipment that she was packing the Prof and Jamie were going to have a very comfortable time even if I was not.

By the time she had me all packed up with clothes and the things in my boot I seemed to be a bit low on my back wheels. I think it must have been the tins of food and the pots and pans she packed that weighed me down so much. I still had no idea where we were going to but then I am not entirely sure that the Prof and Jamie knew either.

I had a real shock when I caught sight of the Prof the next day, I had never seen him like that before, he looked so normal, but then in his own way, which made him not normal. He was wearing tennis shoes and jeans. Well I had never seen him in jeans before, and over the top part of his body he wore a brand new shirt, which actually covered his fat round belly. He wore the shirt un-tucked, so he looked normal; anyway this was his holiday outfit.

I did not have a great deal of work to do on this holiday, it seemed that we were not going very far because we didn't set off very early in the day. We, in fact only went about two or three hours' drive away and soon came to a camp site on the coast.

This coast had very high cliffs, so when Jamie and the Prof went walking on the beach I could not see them.

The Prof really enjoyed his breakfast while he was on this holiday, and every morning he

141

would get up and light the gas first before he even got dressed.

In no time at all he would have a big sizzling plate of bacon, eggs and all the other things humans like to eat. Usually while he was sitting in the sun eating this meal Jamie would wake up to the smell and proceed to make some for himself.

One morning, the two of them were sitting drinking their third cup of tea and discussing what they were to do that day when Jamie suddenly said 'Look Granddad, we have spent the last two weeks doing exactly what I want to do, I have had a great time and met lots of people. We have been to all the pleasure parks, the beaches, the zoos, bowling allies and arcades in the area. I know there is a dig around here somewhere and I know you want to get to it. So let's go shall we?'

'Well as it happens there is a dig in the area but I thought you might be bored if I dragged you along to it.'

'Now let us get this straight' Jamie said in a very stern voice 'It's your holiday as well!'

So that is how the rest of the holiday was spent, my Prof found the dig that Jamie was talking about, it was not very far away. Some days Jamie would come with us and some days he would stay on the site with his friends.

I never did find out exactly what it was they were digging up but I do know that my Prof had a wonderful holiday. I also found out that I had a reason to be grateful to Jamie because on the very last day of the holiday when the two men were packing up the tent and all the other gear my Prof said, 'You know Jamie I was thinking of taking a sabbatical, selling the car and going off to find a dig, but having spent the summer on one I can go back to work at the University with renewed vigour, and it is not too far to pop up here some weekends.'

I must tell you that I breathed a sigh of relief, I did not want to be sold, I liked this Prof and his strange behaviour. Although I was no longer frightened of the thought of being sold, I had got used to my Prof and Duke and Jamie.'

A REALLY EASY RACE

'I hope the bits I ordered arrive in time, even though he has been sprayed there is still loads of work to do before he is finished.' Nick said to Jon.

When Trevor came in he told Gari that he was going with the tractor to collect the new Mini soon.

'Ruth will be pleased.'

'I, too will be pleased, Ruth is asking to drive me all of the time. I wish not to be a snob but I think I do not want her to do the driving of me. I will be too powerful for her.'

'Well that do be the biggest load of ole rubbish I ever did 'ear. I tell you something if that Ruth can drive me then you'd be a piece o' cake for her,' said Trevor.

'And she do a pretty good job of handling me an all Boris, you've got power steering and the likes of that, let's face it you just think she is too young.'

'I think perhaps we should hear some more of Gari's Prof now.' said Boris.

'Yes' I be thinking that I change of subject would be a good idea.'

'I'll tell you what, I will tell you about the time when the Prof gambled me on a race. He was not really a gambling man but this was brought about due to circumstances beyond his control.'

Every evening between the hours of five and seven he would be available to his students so that they could come and talk to him if they had any problems.

One week Johnson came every evening to talk to the Prof, it was obvious that Johnson had a big problem but did not know how to talk about it.

What was the Prof to do, the boy was worried about something and his work was suffering. I heard my Prof and Professor Drummond talking about it. That evening the Prof decided that it had all gone on long enough and he was jolly well going to get to the bottom of it all. As Johnson passed the cottage on his way home from lectures, Prof and Duke, the dog, emerged, as if by accident.

'Ah, Johnson my boy, how about coming for a walk with me and the old dog?'

'Oh yes Professor, it might be quite nice to take a walk, blow away the cobwebs.'

'Right, now then Johnson, I am afraid that I got you in this car under false pretences, while I am driving and Duke is sitting in the front seat there is no way you can get out, so unless you tell me exactly what is bothering you we are going to drive around the country lanes until we run out of petrol. And I have a full tank.'

There was silence in the back for a while, but then Johnson cleared his throat and said,

'Okay Professor, I will tell you but I don't think you can help me.' He took a deep breath and began. 'There is a pub near my digs that I go to, and there is a kid who goes in there who always seems to have loads of money.

Anyway I got friendly with him and we used to play dominos, darts and pool.

Then he said we should put a bet on our games, just to make them more interesting and exciting. At first I refused, I only just about have enough to live on, but as he always seemed to be losing and he had plenty of money anyway I decided that it might supplement my grant.

For a while things went well and I won more than I lost. I don't know if he was playing badly on purpose or if he did genuinely improve as time went on but all of a sudden I began to lose every game and a load of money. He said not to worry, I need not pay it back straight away, it could wait until I got a job.

When he realised that I was only in my first year and wouldn't be getting a job for some years he became very angry and asked for his money back.

Now, Professor he is adding interest, he says that I owe him about £600 and he keeps putting it up each time I see him. I haven't got the money and I cannot pay him.
So Professor, there you have it.'

'You have fallen into a very familiar trap; in fact the same thing happened to me when I was a student.' The Prof told him.

By this time we had got to Duke's exercise place, so the Prof parked me up and they went for their walk. When they came back we drove into a part of the city that I had never seen before, and dropped Johnson off.

'I will come here then at eight-thirty tonight and you will take me to this pub.'

So, at eight-thirty that night, the Prof and I pulled up outside Johnson's digs. He was waiting for us. 'We can walk from here it is not far.'

'I have a feeling that it may be a good idea to take the car, jump in.'

We stopped again just down the road.

'Right I will park here, right outside the pub door, let us go in and imbibe in a small beer.'

From where I was I could see all who entered and left the pub. Presently I caught sight of a young man coming down the road; he looked to be about twenty or so. He wore the most fashionable clothes and his jacket was made of leather. He also had on some very large rings and gold chains hung round his neck.

He stopped and looked closely at me, in fact he was very interested and walked all round me to have a look from all angles, and then he went into the pub.

'So who does the Mini Cooper S belong to?' he called as he went through the door.
Sometime later Johnson and the Prof came out of the pub.

'I can't let you do it Professor; I can't let you race your car against his.'

'The way I see it my boy, is that you do not have a choice in the matter. The deed is done all that remains is for us to set a time for the race, we already know the place.'

'But you bet your car against the debt that means if the race is lost you will lose your car.'

'Also if the race is won, we will be the richer by one car and as I already have a nice one, you can have it. I do not intend to drive the race myself, as it happens I know of someone who can win this race for me, blindfolded.

When we arrived home I was parked outside the open window. I heard the Prof asking for a number on the phone. This number was he told the operator in Ireland, he wanted to speak to a person called Mike Perry. I had heard of this person in fact I knew him quite well from my days with George and Fiona, he was a rally driver. He had won lots of trophies in domestic rallies and abroad as well. I cheered up even more when I heard the Prof ask him to stay and would like to take part in a little private race sometime in the near future. Obviously Perry had said yes because the conversation ended with the Prof saying he would meet the plane.

The race was organised for the next weekend at an old wartime airfield. There was a track all round the airfield which was used for Karts to race round. It was decided to use this track even though it would not be very wide. The Prof found out where this airfield was and drove me out there. He had a good look around and found the track so he decided to have a go around it. The weather had been dry for some time and so the track was not at all muddy or slippery.

He was going faster and faster, he was getting carried away. Coming round one corner he lost control and I spun off the track into a ditch. Luckily it was very shallow at the bit we went in and he was able to drive me out. Good job it wasn't a bit further on because the ditch got deeper there.

There was no damage done but the Prof was a bit shaken up and he was very careful as he drove me slowly home.

On the morning of the race the Prof was to go with me to meet the plane and bring Mike back to the house. The phone rang and I heard the Prof pick it up, 'Oh dear, I am sorry to hear that Mike my boy, I do hope she is not badly hurt. Off a horse you say, and broken her arm. Well she certainly won't feel like flying over today. No; another time. The race? I will have to drive the thing myself. Can't be helped. Oh yes do come next week it will be nice to see you both. Of course I may not be able to pick you up but do come anyway. Goodbye my boy, give your lovely wife my regards and I do hope the break is not too bad.'

It started to rain. It rained very hard, it was pouring down and it just about matched my mood. The rain did not stop and by the time the Prof came out to me to drive to our appointment the road sides were very muddy. We picked up Johnson and I heard the Prof explain to him about Mike not being able to come.

'I have no intention of losing my car,' he told Johnson.

'Forgive me saying so Professor but you did say you had no intention of driving in this race and now you are.'

'This is true: but trust me my boy, trust me.' Well all I could do was to trust my Prof as well and hope he knew what he was doing. When we arrived at the airfield, Lucas and a whole bunch of other people were already there.

Lucas, I should explain was the name of our opponent. The car that he was driving was an Escort, at least it came from the factory as an Escort but this one had all kinds of extra things added to it. It had wide wheels and extra bits on the boot lid. It also had a hole in its bonnet and a see through panel had been dropped into it so that you could see the engine. On his bodywork he had huge red flames painted round his wheel arches.

The Prof pulled up next to this car, got out and went to speak to Lucas. The Escort told me his name was Eddy, he seemed very sure that he was going to win this race and I was pretty sure at the time that he was right, but I was not going to admit that to him.

'Well I think I have a really easy race ahead of me' he said, looking at me with a leering sort of smile. This was not a friendly smile it left me feeling cold.

'Yea? Don't be too sure,' I replied 'You may look as if there is nothing on the road to touch you but it's what's under the bonnet that matters.'

'Well there is plenty under my bonnet, Squirt, I am not standard, you know, I am super tuned.'

'That's fine but do you know how to use all that power, or are you just all throttle and roar? You ever been racing before? Real racing I mean not just this kids stuff. I am an experienced racer and I know how to handle a track, do you?'

'You may have all the experience in the world but how much has your driver had?'

With this parting shot we noticed the humans coming over to us and so we kept quiet. I must say that even though I had tried to sound confident I was really scared that I would lose this race and then I would belong to Lucas.

As we were driving to the starting place I found myself wondering what colour he would paint me and would I have the flames.

We lined up next to each other on the edge of the airfield and a friend of Lucas stood in front of us with his hands in the air. I guessed that the idea was to go on his signal. He dropped his hands and we were away, being careful to give him a wide berth.

The first section of the track was a long straight, I remembered it from the other day when we had driven round, but obviously

Eddy knew it much better, he started to gain on me, his front 'spoiler' just edging ahead. This gave him the advantage at the first corner and here he really pulled in front.

I was annoyed that he had managed to get in front but realised that it was in fact the Prof's inexperience that had allowed it to happen. This was a bad sign and even worse was the fact that Eddy was pulling away from us and the Prof was not making enough speed to catch him. It seemed as if he wanted to loose the race, he didn't seem to be making much effort at all to get past Eddy, I couldn't understand it.

Then we came to a series of bends and some quite sharp corners. Here I had an advantage over Eddy; I was smaller and found the corners easier to take at higher speeds. We gained a bit of speed on the Escort, especially as it was now very wet and muddy. Well we had been round the track once now and I think the Prof had the measure of the race, he began to drive faster and even though we were still behind we were keeping up with Eddy and Lucas.

The Prof did not let any big gaps develop between us on the second lap. In fact I began to realise just what the Prof was doing when I spotted and remembered the ditch that the other day I ended up in.

The ditch was at the end of the last big straight of the track and that made that straight the last good overtaking spot. We were on the straight, and I felt the Prof urging me on. He took me up close to the back of Eddy and just as we went past the half way point of the straight he pulled out and put his foot down on my accelerator, I went with all my power passed Eddy and cut in front of him just as we reached the first bend.

I could see that Lucas was angry at this turn of events and he pressed Eddy's nose close up behind my bumper. He was trying to pass all the time swinging from side to side but the

Prof would not let him through. He also slowed me down to a speed that would just about see me safely around the rest of the track, including the ditch.

This annoyed Lucas even more and he kept ramming me from behind, this hurt but I didn't know if he was doing any real damage. Then Lucas saw a gap and went for it, the Prof let him go and I was happy to do so as well because we knew that at the speed he was going to overtake me he would not make it around the corner, he didn't, he skidded right into the ditch.

Lucas and Eddy were out of the race, the Prof slowed me right down and we crossed the finish line at about ten miles an hour. We stopped and I could see all Lucas' friends helping him out of the car. He came over with Eddy's keys in his hand and threw them at Johnson and said,

'The car is yours but you get it out of the ditch.'

LIKE A HOUSE ON FIRE

So now Gari was green, all over except for his roof. That was still primer grey and also still needed some rubbing down with the very fine paper before Jon could spray it. All in all Gari was beginning to look very respectable.

Lucy popped in every now and again just to see how the job was going.

'Do you think you will have him ready for the classic rally in August?' she asked one day.

'Him?' Nick asked.

'Well seeing him in these colours makes me feel very nostalgic, I think he looks like Gari and it brings back some lovely memories. But I don't suppose I will ever see Gari again; I expect he is long gone.'

Nick found that he could not answer her so he turned to Gari and started to mask up the roof surround, he said 'Well if we don't get this spraying done we will never be ready for the rally.

'Now we have a cream roof and green body work, there is just one more job to be done in the spray booth,' said Jon.

'What is that?' Nick asked.

'A bit of black under the wheel arches to cover up the stone chip, we've done the Clearcoat now and I can bring the wheels home, they're looking very smart and we'll be ready for them tomorrow.' Mark was sitting in Lenny's driver seat, on his way to work. Jon had no jobs in that day and was determined to get the paint work finished on Gari.

'Right little car, let's get you finished off, when Marc comes home with your wheels tonight you can come off those axel stands and stand on brand new tyres.'

With that Jon started up the compressor and filled the under seal gun with black paint.

Spraying the wheel arches did not take long and while Jon was waiting for it to dry he started to polish Gari's body.

'Hmm this has got to be the best of all' thought Gari.

'I will have a lovely shine by the time Jon has finished.'

And indeed he did shine. Lucy remarked upon it when she came in with Boris that evening.

'Oh Jon, he looks great.'

'Not bad is it, think I did a good job then, Mum?'

'You know I do, I was just saying to your dad the other day that he reminds me of Gari, but then you wouldn't know about that I sold him to Uncle George before you were born.'

Gari looked out of the door and saw Lenny pulling to a standstill outside the barn. Marc hopped down and walked round the back, from there he heaved a wheel. Ruth came from the house and pulled another one down, Lucy fetched one and Jon another. Immediately Marc brought in the trolley jack and they put all four wheels onto Gari. They then all pushed him out of the little room into the big part of the barn.

Oh, Gari did feel good, he was bright and shiny, he was in a large space and all his people were standing around looking at him, proudly, especially Lucy who he still loved right down to the bottom of his brand new, pumped up tyres.

Boris, Lenny and Trevor still managed to fit into the barn okay but there was not much room as before and Lucy had to be a bit careful of Boris's doors when she opened them. The other vehicles were most impressed with Gari's new appearance. When they had finished admiring him, Boris, who was feeling a touch jealous said he wanted to hear more of Gari's time with the Prof.

'Well as I am in a happy mood I will tell you about the wedding shall I?'

'What wedding do that be then Boy, who went an got married then?' asked Trevor.

'Both of the professors. You see Mrs Green was a widow, she and Professor Drummond began to 'walk out''.

My Prof was very pleased for his friend and liked Mrs Green; in fact he was happy for them both and invited them both round to his cottage to share a meal sometimes. He joked that if they were to get together that would be the only way he was ever going to get another decent meal.

One day Professor Drummond told my Prof that he had a visitor arriving the next day, he was to meet the train but also had lectures, could my Prof go instead.

'Who is coming old chap? I must be sure that I collect the right person.'

'My sister Diana, she is coming to live with me for a while. You have met her before I believe.'

'Oh, Indeed I have, I remember her coming to stay before, and what does the delectable Mrs G think of all this?'

'She seems quite happy about it but then she does not know Diana, and doesn't believe me when I tell her just how exasperating Diana can be. She has lost her house you see, she bet it on a 'dead cert' as she puts it, and lost.'

I must explain to you about Diana, she was Professor Drummond's youngest sister. I gained the impression that the good Professor did not entirely approve of his sister.

She lived, in Yorkshire, she had a nice cottage in a small village where she had lived since her last husband left her. She had three husbands but they had all either left her or had died.

'She can earn herself a very good living with her painting; she paints water colours which she sells very successfully. But as soon as she is comfortable money wise she goes running off and starts betting again.

To give her her dues she often wins but when she does lose she will lose everything, as she has this time.' Professor Drummond explained.

'I expect she is a bit upset now!' my Prof inquired.

'Not at all, old boy, she takes it all in her stride, in fact it never seems to bother her, just makes it very inconvenient for me, especially now that I have Edith to think of. I was going to ask Edith to marry me, but how can I expect her to share the house with Diana?'

'Marry you? Well here I was thinking that you would never get married, but then Mrs Green is a very good cook.'

'I am not marrying her for her culinary expertise, Cargill, I happen to have fallen for the lady.'

'Don't get all upset now, I was only joking, so what time do you want me to meet this train?'

'Three o'clock.'

When I saw Diana I was amazed, she was nothing like I expected. Professor Drummond always dressed in smart suits in dark colours, in a very conservative manner. Diana was dressed in a flamboyant way; she was about forty-five years old and had very blonde hair. It was long and curly. She wore it up in a sort of bun' but not much of it had stayed up, there were curls sticking out all over the place, but it didn't look messy, untidy, but right somehow. She was wearing a very big brimmed hat that flopped down almost to her shoulders so I didn't see her hair until she took her hat off. Her coat was very long; it came down to her ankles and was made of material that looked like curtains, you know, flowery. Under this I could see she had on a black dress that had no shape to it and was also quite long but not so that it hid the gold boots she wore.

She clinked and clanked as she walked because she was wearing an enormous amount of plastic jewellery. There were about twenty bracelets on each wrist and round her neck were lots and lots of chains and strings of beads.

Hanging from one shoulder she had a huge bag, a big floppy thing which hung on a long strap and reached her knees, and she had slung round her hips three or four belts. I am not sure how many there were but she looked as if she was actually wearing every piece of jewellery and all the belts she owned.

When she took off her hat I saw that she was wearing a long scarf tied round her head so that the ends hung down her back, but it didn't cover her hair.

I couldn't see her face very well because she had on a giant pair of sunglasses which covered her up most successfully. I must say she didn't look very upset.

'Well I think Drummond is more perturbed about it all than I am' she was saying. 'I'm afraid that I'm disturbing his arrangements somewhat but I won't disrupt him for long, I will be back on my feet in no time, you'll see. Anyway it is so nice to see you again Roland have you been keeping well? Oh is this your car? What a sweet little thing, he has a name as well I see, how marvellous. I will call him after his number, Gari. Do you call him that or am I being rather too obvious?'

'Well I can't say I have thought about it but you are right he should have a name and Gari it shall be from now on.'

'Do you still have the dog Drummond wrote to me about?'

'Yes; but I left Duke at home, he takes up rather a lot of room in the car and I didn't know how much luggage you would have with you.'

'Well, as you can see, I travel light, some clothes and my painting stuff, the rest I fear is in storage.'

I noticed that when she talked she also used her arms a lot, waving them about with her words, in fact she was always on the move, even on the drive home she moved about in her seat, first this way then that, I think you could say she was a very expressive lady.

After a few days we were so used to having Diana around it felt as if she had always been there, she would spend most of her days painting pictures of the cottages, the college, the grounds and even me.

My Prof would spend some time just sitting and talking to her while she painted. On one morning in particular, they were sitting in the garden when I saw Diana jump up and give the Prof a big hug and a kiss.

'Oh Roland, how kind of you.' I wondered what he had done that was so kind and I found out that afternoon when Diana, shouldering her big bag came to me with my keys in her hand.

This was the beginning of a period of exploration around the countryside for us both. Diana was looking for nice scenery to paint. I thought that this was rather familiar and it reminded me of the time with Stephen, but there was a difference in that we went to different places and Diana painted what she saw and not what was in her mind.

On the way out of Cambridge we would very often pass a betting shop and it was not long before we began to make a stop at this place. We would sometimes stop there on the way back as well and when we did Diana would be particularly bubbly and happy. Diana had taken to carrying a small portable radio with her to listen to while she was painting.

One day we stopped at an electrical shop and from there we went to a garage. Diana had bought a car radio and it was to be fitted in. this meant that wherever she was she could listen to the racing results. I wondered what my Prof would say about this, but he didn't mind at all. 'What a good idea,' was all he said.

As the weeks went by I noticed that Diana and my Prof were spending more and more time together, sometimes when Diana was out painting the Prof would come and either bring a book with him or they would spend time just talking. In the winter we would still go out but Diana didn't paint, she had a camera and took photographs of places, from which she would do paintings at home. Most often she did these pictures in my Prof's cottage rather than at Professor Drummond's, in fact I could see through the window her easel set up in the lounge and all her paints and brushes fighting for space on the table with the Prof's books.

'Cargill. Cargill.' Professor Drummond was running, yes running from his cottage. I looked at Ian and the Imp in pure puzzlement but he just said 'Wait and see'.

Diana and Roland came out to see what was wrong, they looked very worried but they soon smiled when Professor Drummond spilled out his news.

'I asked her, Edith, I asked her to marry me.'

'And?'

'And she said yes!'

At this point Edith appeared in the doorway to be greeted with the sight of Diana rushing to her arms flung wide.

'How wonderful, Drummie and you getting married, oh I am so pleased for you both.'

Diana then grabbed Edith into her arms and did a dance on the front door step. Edith looked rather embarrassed by this show of affection but then Diana was a very theatrical person, all her actions were larger than life. Ian looked smug and I could tell he knew all about it but I did wonder how he knew that

Edith would say yes. He said he just knew so I left it at that. Once Diana had calmed down a bit my Prof cleared his throat.

'Hrumph, well what do you think then Diana, do you think we could er, make it a-er, double wedding? That is if the two of you don't mind sharing your day of glory.'

'You want to marry Diana?' Professor Drummond was incredulous.

'I do, indeed I do,' replied The Prof.

I had never seen Diana so still; she stood there with Edith still in her arms, just staring with her mouth open. Then very slowly she let her arms fall and walked sedately over to my Prof, there she stood for what must have been a full minute. I stole a look at my Prof who was standing waiting for a reply; he was holding his breath I think. Then quietly and calmly Diana said 'Thank you, Roland, I would like to marry you.'

It was said so quietly that at first I didn't think that the Prof had heard her but then he smiled. 'Champagne, we should have champagne for an occasion such as this' he yelled and off we went to the shops to get some.

The wedding was a month later; Ian and I were all decked out with white ribbons for the day. On the morning of the wedding both the Professors' dressed in their best suits and got into Ian. A few moments later the ladies emerged from Prof Drummond's cottage, Edith looked very smart in a neat navy blue suit with a small hat perched on top of her head. Diana wore a long flowing grey coloured dress, a bright red floppy hat, red shoes and hundreds or red bead necklaces.

They made themselves comfortable inside me and Diana drove us to the Registry Office for the ceremony. It was supposed to be a very quiet occasion but by the time the four people came out of the office there were about a hundred students standing around Ian and me who all gave a huge cheer. There was a lot of talking but eventually we set off very slowly.

The students had told my Prof and Professor Drummond to follow them, well as they were all on push bikes that made the going slow. There we were driving along surrounded by bikes ridden by cheering students, I felt as if we were in a carnival procession. Eventually we found out where the students were taking us, it turned out to be the dining hall of the college.

When we parked, Ian and I were speechless because our two professors and their new wives were carried shoulder high into the college. Ian and I didn't see them again until much later that night.'

THE CARGILL DIG

Gari stood in the barn feeling a bit depressed; he couldn't understand why Marc had taken off his nice shiny bonnet. He cheered up when he watched Lenny backing into the barn because on the back he could see his engine. Marc brought Lenny to a standstill under a beam from which was hanging some ropes and the pulley contraption that they had used to take the engine out.

Marc and Jon tied some ropes to the pulley and then round the engine, then Jon pulled on one rope and the engine lifted up while Marc drove Lenny out again. Jon tied the rope off and both of them came to Gari, they pushed him so that his engine compartment was under the beam. And then, oh Gari was so excited, they lowered the engine into the compartment. Gari felt the weight push down his front end so that he was level again and not always looking up in the air.

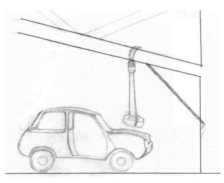

It felt so good, so very nice. Jon and Marc made themselves busy bolting the brackets in place and connecting the drive shafts and the gears all together.

There were lots of other bolts, tubes and wires to fix in place and this took some time but finally the ropes were off and Gari's internal workings were all in place.

Then came two sorts of different oils, some for the gear box and engine and some for the brakes, which was called fluid, and poured into the special little holes which were then plugged with their own little plugs.

All the time this was going on Jon kept saying, 'Mind the paintwork, don't let's scratch it now.'

Ruth came into the barn and said,

'Are you going to start it up and make sure it goes properly?'

'What ever do you mean make sure? We'll put some petrol in and I will prove to you what a good mechanic I am,' Marc replied.

Gari felt the liquid running down the short pipe into his petrol tank, it felt to him like us having a cold drink of water on a hot summer's day. He had not realised how thirsty he was until he had that drink. Jon found a box to put inside Gari's cab so that Marc could sit inside because there were no seats in there as yet. A few pumps on the accelerator pedal to push the fuel through and then he pushed the starter button, but nothing happened.

Both Marc and Jon yelled at the same time 'The battery'. They had forgotten to put it in and connect it up.

'My brothers, the master mechanics,' scoffed Ruth.

The two of them were rather embarrassed but they soon got over it and found the new battery that Nick had brought for Gari.

'Instead of standing there taking the mickey why don't you go and get those new carpets that I brought home yesterday,' Marc suggested to Ruth.

'I will when you have got him started and not before.'

With that she stood up straight and folded her arms, waiting. Marc tried again and after a couple of tries the engine came to life. Gari giggled around in excitement but the people didn't notice; they were all cheering. Lucy walked in and gained the impression that her children had all gone stark staring mad, but she soon joined in the party when she heard Gari's engine running.

'The timing needs sorting out and one or two other adjustments and it will purr like a pussy cat,' Marc said when he had calmed down a bit.

'Now Ruth will you go and get those carpets?'

'Sure thing master mechanic brother.'

'I came to tell you that the tea is ready and I think you had better switch him off so as not to tire him too much on his first day' Lucy said.

'Sometimes I wonder about you Mother' Ruth laughed and with that Trevor chugged in with Nick.

'You've got him going, that's great' exclaimed Nick as he jumped down.

'I'll do some fine tuning tomorrow but mum says its tea time now,' Marc said turning off the engine and with that all the humans went off chattering to eat their tea.

'How about that then Trevor, I have a working engine again, it can't be long now before I can go and drive people about again.'

'That do be real good, Boy they got you done quicker than I did think.'

'It's been such a long time since my engine ran I thought it never would go again, but it does, it's brilliant.'

'There only be one way you'll calm down Boy an that be for you to tell me some more bout that there Prof of yours, else I won't be getting no rest this night that's for sure.'

'Okay I will calm down for now I can get excited again tomorrow,' giggled Gari.

'Life,' he said proudly 'with the Prof and Diana carried on after they were married as it had before, I spent most of my time going round the countryside with Diana, but no more visits to the betting shops.

Duke even took to sitting in the back so that Diana could put her painting gear on the front seat, because he came with us most of the time, and after a quick run around he would settle down to sleep while she was painting. It proved a little difficult to persuade him to use the back seat when Prof was driving, he was so used to sitting in the front, but he gave in eventually.

The three of them still went for walks each morning, but one morning there was something different about the place but I couldn't tell what at first. It was the Prof who told us what it was. 'A supermarket?'

There was a big notice board up and the Prof read out what it said, 'They are going to build a supermarket and some other shops here, that's a shame it looks as if we are going to have to find somewhere else to walk the dog.'

'Well they are not going to start right away in fact not till next year. At least it is not far away to do the shopping and it will be better than driving into Cambridge all the time.'

We carried on going to this place and the notices got more and more numerous, the supermarket was to be Sainsways and there was to be a chemist shop, a bakery, a newsagents shop, a hairdressers and one or two others which did not have a business in them yet.

The date was fast approaching when the work was due to start and one day when we arrived the place was fenced off and we couldn't get in. this didn't stop Duke, he went over the fence and had a nose around at all the vehicles that were parked there.

There were diggers and dumper trucks all standing around waiting to start work. The ground had been marked in large shapes with piles of sand.

We went off to find somewhere else to walk Duke, but the Prof said he was very interested in the building and wanted to come back every day to see how it was coming on.

So each day we would stop and have a look, after a few days all the piles of sand had disappeared and there were deep holes in place of them. Duke ran off to investigate the holes and have a general sniff around but one day he came back limping. When the Prof and Diana looked there was a sharp stone bedded in his pad. They took him home and bandaged him up.

The Prof seemed very interested in the stone, it was not in fact a stone but flint and it was not just a chip of flint but part of a knife. I knew this because I heard him yell it when he had looked it up in some of his books.

He phoned up some people he knew who came over straight away to look at the knife. They all agreed that the building must be stopped because there were obviously some remains of great importance down there, and it could be destroyed by the work.

Well then we were off again the Prof and one of his friends, back to the site. We parked and the Prof was off and running across the land closely followed by another man and Duke.

The builders must have had a shock when they saw these three running towards them, the Prof yelling that they must stop work.

'Sorry mate this is private land, can't come in ere, you'll have to go.'

'But you don't understand you are working on an important archaeological site, you could be destroying vital evidence of historical interest. You have to stop; where is the site manager; I must speak to him.'

A man came out of a large caravan and walked over to where the Prof was standing.

'I am the foreman here, what is the problem?'

'You have to stop work, we have found a flint knife blade from this site and we must have a chance to investigate it before you ruin it all with your diggers.'

By the time the Prof had said all this there were three more cars parked beside me and students from our college piled out of them. These young people went and sat down in front of the diggers and effectively brought the work to a complete standstill.

'Look I don't know who you are but if I were you I would get out of here and take all these kids with you, we have work to do here and if you don't move I will have to get the police in to clear you all out.'

Even as he was saying this more and more students were arriving. I saw the man going back into the caravan and quite soon after the first of the police cars arrived, with blues and twos blaring.

This poor man couldn't do much on his own because by this time there must have been hundreds of students sitting around the building site. I wondered how they all knew about it but I didn't let it worry me unduly. I only began to get worried when some more policemen arrived and took the Prof away in a patrol car.

The students stayed where they were and the angry builders were stomping around totally unable to get on with their holes. We had been sitting there for about three and a half hours when a Rolls Royce arrived and a very important looking man got out of the back of it. He went to talk to the foreman and they had a discussion which included a good deal of arm waving and shouting. Then he walked, or rather marched, back to his car and was driven away by the chauffer.

Sometime later he arrived back at the site with the Prof and they went to a pile of dirt near one of the diggers where the Prof got down on his hands and knees and started shovelling it about with his hands. He very soon stopped and brought out something which he showed to the important man. I heard him say that it could be a small dumping ground or it could be the site of a complete stone age village, either way it was vital that he should be allowed to dig it and find out. The important looking man was interested despite himself but he said,

'You can have no concept of how much money will be lost if this project is not finished on time. It could run into the millions.'

'But think of the cost to the nation if this find is lost forever under tons of concrete.' The argument went on for hours but in the end the important looking man said he would try and see if he could raise any grants to cover the cost, and he mentioned something about insurance but the Prof was not to move in and start digging until he heard from the man.

The Prof looked a bit dubious but agreed to this, meanwhile the students had worked a rota system so that some of them could stay and guard the holes all the time. The Prof came away then with promises of refreshment and sleeping bags for those that were staying on.

When we got home we found Diana had been busy as well, as we were pulling up outside the house, the front door opened and lots of ladies came out.

'Roland, meet the dig committee, these good ladies here are all experienced fund raisers and with their help we can raise some of money needed to carry out the Cargill find.'

Every day we went to the site and the Prof sifted through the earth that had already been brought out of the holes and found bits of flint that could have been tools, but he kept his word and didn't do any digging. One day, some weeks after the Rolls came again and the important looking man got out but this time he did not look so important. In fact he was dressed in jeans and a very old jumper.

He went over to the Prof and shook hands with him. I couldn't hear what they were saying but the Prof seemed very happy and slapped the man on the back in his joy.

It seemed that we had a dig. Somehow this man had arranged it so that they had a whole year to dig the site before the builders came back and then, no matter what was left there, the supermarket had to be built. He also was going to help with the dig because he was very interested to find out what was down there. His name, by the way was Neville Lacey, and I got to know him quite well.

He came to the dig every weekend for the whole year; he never missed a single one.

Anyway for the first few weeks the dig was rather boring because it took a long time to dig down to the right level, but then the diggers started to find bits of pot and tools.

The Prof said that what they had was a big Neolithic house which was built of wood. He said the trees were cut down with axes that the people here had brought from traders, who had come from North Wales. That seemed to me an awful long way to travel especially as they didn't have any cars then.

Apparently these people were some of the first farmers and they grew crops and kept cattle. They all lived together in one big house, the people and the cattle and dogs, and they even stored the grain in there as well.

Everything that came out of the holes was carefully cleaned, photographed and given a number; they then were stored in wooden trays.

Diana was often there making paintings of pieces of pottery and things, and some of the people spent their time piecing together the bits of pottery. It looked like they were doing a three dimensional jigsaw.

One day Diana and the Prof were sitting in my cab eating a sandwich lunch when Diana said 'It seems such a shame to put all these things in a museum with a load of others, is it not possible to make this place into an attraction of some kind? I was thinking that we could rebuild it as it was in Neolithic times and charge people to come and see it.'

'It's a nice thought; I could have a word with Neville and see if it could be done. The actual building is not very far under the foundations in fact most of it is in the car park, but I expect he will have a very good reason why it can't be done.'

Neville didn't have any reason why it couldn't be done; he had been thinking along the same lines himself and had already approached the parish council and the architect to arrange planning permission. He had also been talking to other companies for funding to create such a project.

'The way I see it, Roland is that I should be able to find the money to do it but there is an added problem in that this structure would take up half the car park, so we will need more land to accommodate the cars. It all rests on how much money we could make out of it.'

My Prof was not terribly interested in the money side of the project; he was more concerned with finding out and teaching people about the lifestyle of Neolithic Man. If this could be done, it was just possible that when the year was up the digging would not have to stop. Well I don't know exactly what happened, I do know that my Prof went to lots of meetings with or without Neville, sometimes Diana went with him.

One night he came home from a meeting very late in the Rolls, Neville got out and went to the boot from which he lifted a big box of champagne. They went into the house and I heard Diana squeal with delight when they told her that the deal was done and they could build the museum. I saw them through the window, standing in the lounge touching glasses before they took a drink, and I must say I felt very smug.

Meanwhile the digging was still going on and my Prof and I spent many days at the site. Diana was doing lots of drawings of what the Prof thought the house would look like inside and out. Eventually the dig was cleaned out and it was done before the year was finished as well, all the bits taken from it had been catalogued and recorded either by photograph or a painting from Diana and so it was time to start drawing up plans for the building. It took another two years to get the building done but when it was finished I felt very special because I had my own parking space with my name written on the wall.'

OUT TO PASTURE

There were only a few more jobs left to be done to Gari, his seats were back in and he had some brand new carpets. Nick and Jon had spent a whole day putting all his windows in place and he had his front grille in as well.

All he needed now was his bumpers, all the chrome trimmings, his number plates and of course his badge.

Every time Nick came into the barn he fetched a soft cloth and gave Gari a gentle rub, the he stood back to admire the shine.

'Well Dad, we did it, have you entered him into the Classic Car Rally?'

'Yup, sent off the entry form last week. We have plenty of time to finish the little jobs before I give him back to your mother. I hope she is pleased with him after all this work.'

'She will be, she keeps coming into the barn to have a quiet look at him when she thinks no one is about, I am sure she knows that you are going to give Gari to her. I just hope she has not suspected who he is.'

'She nearly found out the other day when I left the number plates in Boris but I think I got them out without her seeing them.'

Gary asked Trevor. 'Did Nick say when he was going to bring the new mini in; you know the one that they are going to do up for Ruth?'

'Arr, that be coming about time of the rally, Nick an I be going to get it on that Saturday. It's not in such bad nick as you was but that Isn't a runner like, it's got some problem with its motor see.'

'I know the feeling; by the time I left the Prof I had some problems with my bits and pieces as well.'

'How long was you all together then?'

'Over ten years in all, then I failed my M.O.T test and the Prof had accepted a job abroad so he sold me. But I still had a few years to enjoy my own personal parking place. The Prof decided that he didn't have time to catalogue all the treasures that they had dug up and carry on with his lectures. So once the museum was built he left the University to work full time on his findings. He also wanted to write two books, one on what he found, a sort of text book, and one was to be the story of the dig. He said that this would be an inspiration to anyone who finds remains that they think are worth digging.

Well all this meant that he and Diana had to move out of the cottage because it belonged to the University and went with the job.

We went to live in a house Diana found near the dig site.

For some weeks Diana and I went all over the nearby country-side looking at houses. I was quite taken with some of them because they had nice cosy looking garages but Diana did not like many of them enough to bring the Prof to look.

By this time I found it difficult to get going in the morning, and sometimes my engine just didn't want to start. I felt much better when I could go in the garage at night. I was also pleased that I didn't have to go so far with the Prof each day or ramble around the countryside with Diana; she now did much of her painting at home.

In fact sometimes I didn't have to leave my cosy garage at all because the Prof liked to walk across the fields to the museum and he took Duke with him.

I didn't know what was wrong with me but when I did go out I never seemed to have the energy that I once had, I began to find the hills hard to climb and any long journeys made me very tired. I also seemed to need more petrol and oil than I ever had before.

Whenever Diana or the Prof started up my engine a great puff of blue smoke would come out of my exhaust and I would cough and splutter for a long while until I had warmed up.

As the weather began to get colder, and the Prof used me more to go to work, I found even that short journey tired me out. One day I just couldn't get my engine to start, I tried very hard to start but I kept coughing and nothing happened.

The Prof left me in the garage and went back indoors. I saw him come out again all wrapped up in his cloak and a big scarf and with his big black hat on his head he set off to walk across the fields. Later on that day I watched as a tow truck pulled into the yard. The man got out and went to speak to Diana, then backed the tow truck up to the garage doors and hooked me up to it.

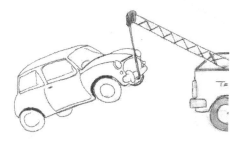

I was so embarrassed, I had been towed places before, after the accident with Stephen and at various other times but never because I was ill. I felt that the whole world was watching me as the tow truck took me to the garage.

When we arrived it was even worse because we had to go past a sales pitch which was populated with cars that were all newer and in better condition than me.

They all looked as we went past and there I was with my front wheels dangling in mid air. I heard them laughing at me. I felt so old and sad I think I must have been crying because when the mechanic came to look at me he noticed some water under my headlights. Later that day Diana arrived to take me back home and I found that I could start my engine again and in fact I felt much better but I never did have the energy that I was used to having.

Not long after my last visit to the garage I saw an Escort drive into the driveway, with the Prof at the wheel. He parked it in the garage beside me, and I realised that it was one of the cars that was laughing at me the day I broke down.

I did not go out much after that, only on warm days when my engine would be able to start properly. Diana would take me into town sometimes but they mostly used the Escort.

He was a young sporty car who thought a lot of himself and never wasted an opportunity to have a go at me. How old and useless I was, how they were going to get rid of me. Let me rot away. He told me of all the places he had taken the Prof, trying to make me jealous. I didn't mind, although I never told him but I was quite happy sitting in the garage and only going out on sunny days. It suited me fine.

Then it happened again. My world came crashing down around me. The Prof and Diana decided to live abroad to pursue more digs that the Prof had heard of.

The Escort was to be sold and I would be going for scrap. At least that is what he told me. It didn't happen like that I was actually given to a couple of boys that lived on a farm. They wanted a car to ride around the fields in.

Tommy and Jake, to their credit did some repairs to me and made me feel a bit stronger again before they thrashed me around the farm. Every time a bit of me broke they would have to go and earn some money to repair me again. So I spent more time broken than I did running. The work they did to me was all very make piece and bodged but it worked and sometimes I felt very well and full of energy. I enjoyed my time with the boys but eventually they got fed up and left me in a barn.

I did not see them for some time a couple of years at least by which time the chickens had taken up residence. I was slowly rotting away into a gentle peaceful death. I was never lonely because the chickens were always so noisy during the day and kept me warm at night when they roosted on my seats, back parcel shelf, foot wells, and even the front dash board.

That's where I stayed, and until I thought I saw Nick one day I was happy to just fade away. I would often wonder at what point a car actually died.

Then there was that awful day that I thought I was going to be crushed.

The day that turned into a really good one, when Nick came to save me and I came here and met all of you.

HELLO GARI

The day of the rally dawned bright and sunny. Gari was clean, bright and shiny. Ruth came into the barn with the ignition key, and started him up.

She drove Gari out of the barn and parked him in front of the house. Nick stood waiting there with a big parcel in his hands which he unwrapped. Gari saw that it was a long piece of red cloth. Ruth and Nick passed the cloth under Gari and brought the ends up either side of him. They tied a big red bow on his roof.

'Where's Mum?' Ruth asked.

'The boys are keeping her busy in the kitchen but I think we can present Gari to her now if you would like to go and get her.'

Gari was shaking with excitement. At last Lucy would know he was here, that the car that had stood in the barn all these weeks was the very first car she had owned.

He was also going to see his old friend Maurice today because that day was the 25th of August the day of the big rally. It was Nick and Lucy's wedding anniversary. It was the day he had been waiting for. He could hardly contain himself and now the time had come. He would be with Lucy again, properly as her car, for ever.

There she was, coming out of the front door.

'Oh! The Mini, it's for me? It looks great; you have all done a wonderful job.'

Lucy walked around the car looking closely at him while Gari shook uncontrollably. She got to Nick who was standing in front of Gari and was smiling like a little boy. She looked at Gari again and caught sight of his number plate. Lucy let out a loud squeal and turned to hug Nick. 'It's Gari! It's really him.' she cried jumping up and down on the spot.

There were hugs and tears all around and lots of talking while Nick explained where he had found Gari and how they all kept the secret from Lucy just so she could receive her car on this special day.

'I will never trust a word you say, ever again, all of you. How could you have kept this secret form me all these months?'

Eventually the humans were all ready to leave for the rally. Lucy was to drive Gari with Nick as her passenger and the children all got into Boris.

Gari saw Maurice as soon as he turned into the field and was overjoyed to note that they would be parked together.

As the days events went on and Gari went out on his drive with Marc and Jon he had the feeling that he could see people that he knew. Then it happened, Gari saw George and Fiona. In itself, that would not be unusual because as family they were often visiting the farm. But then an elderly gentleman walked over to them and introduced himself to the family.

'Cargill is the name,' he greeted them with a handshake. 'This is my wife Diana.'

Nick turned and shook hands with the gentleman and said 'Glad you could come. Do you remember the car then?'

'He looks tremendous, just like a new car.' Diana said, 'I am so glad we were in England for this and to meet up with this little car again.'

Gari was positively tingling with pleasure and all through the day he saw again most the people that had driven him through his life. Nick had tracked them all down and managed to get them all together for this his special day. The only person who was missing was Steve. Trish was there and she told a sad story of Steve. He had been killed in a bad accident. Apparently he never could stop taking the drugs. That news made Gari very sad and for a while he thought he would cry. In fact he did have a few tears and Lucy saw his lights were wet.

She did not say anything but she patted his bonnet just so that he would know she had noticed. It made him feel better but it was still very sad and Gari thought it was such a waste of a life.

Those drugs had a lot to answer for.

Nick invited everybody back to the farm for a barbeque and later that evening all Gari's people were gathered outside his barn, eating and chatting about him. All of them, swapping stories and jokes. It was a lovely evening and Gari thought only one thing would make it perfect. There was someone missing.

Monica, if only she could be here to enjoy this day with him. He was chatting away to Maurice and reminiscing about the times they had been together as young cars. Maurice told him that he had never left his home and led a quiet life now, only coming out to days like these and how nice it was to be able to meet up with him again.

Gari heard the blast of a horn and Trevor pulled into the yard pulling the trailer.

Gari could not see from where he was what was on the trailer but very soon all the men had untied the ropes and were all pulling and heaving a small car down the ramps and pushing it into the barn.

'My next project,' Nick announced proudly. Oh that's nice, Gari thought. Nick is going to give another car a new chance of a happy life. The car was pushed in beside Gari and slightly forward of him. He could then see that it was a white mini. There were see red seats in the car and when he looked closely he was astonished.

'Hello Gari.' Monica said.

Dear Reader

If you have enjoyed reading this book, then please leave a review on Amazon.

Thank you.

About the Author

Diana has always wanted to write and has throughout her life jotted down little poems and short stories.

She has spent a good deal of her working life in the employment of the Citizens' Advice Bureau, mainly as a debt counsellor.

After retiring last year, Diana hoped to have more time to write and wrote a piece which was published in 'View of the Sea', an anthology to raise money for Alzheimer's Research UK.

If you would like to keep up to date with Diana's writing you can follow her on Facebook:
https://www.facebook.com/Diana-Bettinson-Author-page-158069648021521/

Printed in Great Britain
by Amazon